THE WARRIOR

and the

MISCHIEVOUS WITCH

Maggie Carpenter

ADULT ADVISORY

This book is for adults only, and contains scenes of spanking, graphic sex, bondage, sensory deprivation, and are fantasies only, intended for adults. This book is not for children, nor does it condone corporal punishment of children. This book contains scenes of nonconsensual activities, BDSM and other nonconsensual activities. This book does not support nonconsensual spanking or any other nonconsensual activities, sexual or otherwise.

This book is a work of fiction. The characters, incidents, and dialogue are drawn from the author's imagination and are not to be construed as real. Any resemblance to actual events or persons, living or dead is entirely coincidental.

Published by Dark Secrets Press

DARK SECRETS PRESS

ISBN: 978-0692418048

Cover Design: Ashley@ Redbird Designs
Formatting: Polgarus Studio

Visit the author at:
www.Amazon.com/author/maggiecarpenter
www.maggiecarpenter.com
www.MaggieCarpenter.com/blog
www.facebook.com/MaggieCarpenterWriter
www.twitter.com/magcarpenter2

CONTENTS

CHAPTER ONE

Angelica laughed merrily as she darted through the woods. Though some would chastise her for what she'd done, she saw it as her duty. The little boy deserved it. She'd seen him tease the animals in the forest too many times, and now he was sorry.

It had been a simple spell, and for a young witch with such great skill and inherited power it had required only an incantation. When the child had begun poking the porcupine with a stick, she had hummed the words and sent them on their way.

Mean little child, be mean no more
If you continue, you will soon be sore
You will fall quickly and skin your knee
So I ask it, so it shall be
Each time, every time, that you cause pain
You will fall down, again and again.

At some point he'd make the connection; hurt an animal, he'd trip over and be hurt in return. It was fair, it was justice, and it would stop him.

She'd had a pleasant dance through the woods, but as she neared her cottage she felt a presence. Pausing, she dropped the hood of her cape and tilted her head.

The presence was male, strong, pure of heart, and he was waiting for her. Taking a breath and closing her eyes she attempted read him, learn the message he had or what favor he might be asking, but to her surprise and disappointment she felt nothing.

Strange. How is he blocking me? No-one can block me, not unless he has a sorcerer helping him. Perhaps he does, though I don't smell one.

A sorcerer would use oils or plants to thwart the senses of a witch, but she detected no such aromatic protection.

Filled with curiosity she hurried forward, skirting the perimeter of her house, and though she could feel him nearby he wasn't in sight. Raising her arms above her head she let her fingertips touch the air.

Ah, a warrior. He is a warrior, and he has the stealth of a warrior. He is to the side and behind me.

Slowly turning around, still shrouded in the woodsy mist, she leaned against a tree trunk and smiled.

"You may come out, warrior. I know you are there, and I know you wish me no harm. I will take you into my cottage and brew you some tea, a tea you will enjoy and that will nourish your body."

The tall, heavily muscled man stepped from the shadows, his sword gleaming at his side.

"Your senses are as keen as I was told," he declared in a voice thick and deep. "I wonder, Angelica, are the other things I've heard about you also true?"

"Since I don't know what you've been told, I don't know the answer to that question. You'll just have to find out for yourself," she quipped. "Do you wish to come into my house and have tea?"

"I was told you can be very mischievous, that you don't always listen to those you should," he continued not allowing her to change the subject.

"Just because someone thinks they know better than me, it doesn't mean they do," she retorted. "I'm going inside now. You're welcome to join me, but you must take my hand as we walk through my garden to the front door."

"I've heard about that too," *and you are as capricious as my Prince said you were.*

Moving closer, he wished he could see her more clearly. The mist around her was like a white veil, transparent, but allowing no detail to show through.

"I was told to wait for you out here, that no man, woman or even another witch, can enter through your gate and reach your door without feeling faint. No-one seems to know how you do it, not even other witches."

"No-one shall," she said firmly. "It is my protective spell, and sharing its secrets will lessen its potency. Are you joining me, or are you going to stay out here?"

"Thank you, Angelica, I'd be delighted to join you."

"Your name?"

"My name is Darius."

"Darius, a good, strong name. You are welcome in my home."

He knew she was gifted with extraordinary talent, but he'd also been told she could be unpredictable. Still wary of their meeting he continued stepping slowly towards her.

"Please don't fear me," she said softly, sensing his trepidation. "I only hurt those that hurt me, or cause malicious pain to others."

"You can read me already?" he muttered somewhat unnerved, *and how your voice changed when you said that. You sounded almost vulnerable.*

"Of course I can read you," she replied, *but not as much as most, or as much as I would like.*

She stepped out of the mist, and he discovered her loveliness had not been exaggerated. Her deep purple eyes shone, and her dark hair against her pale skin and red lips gave her the look of a fine porcelain statuette. Dressed in a pink and white, diaphanous gown that floated like a cloud around her body, he could detect her luscious figure as the fine fabric lightly touched various parts of her. The black cape fell behind her shoulders, exaggerating the lightness of the dress, and he thought it almost like a picture frame surrounding her beauty. Extending his hand he felt her fine fingers slip into his palm, and as they curled around his, a subtle tingle traveled up his arm.

"Come, Darius. We will drink tea, share some rosemary honey on bread, and you will tell me why you're here."

"You don't know?" he challenged.

"Ah, you want to play that game. Very well," she sighed.

"I'm sorry," he apologized, "have I upset you?"

"It happens often, people wanting to test me. It does become tiresome."

They had reached the front door of the thatched roof cottage, and to his amazement it swung open of its own accord.

"Do you hail from Zanderone?" she asked.

"Yes, I do," he replied his eyes scanning the room as they entered.

"Are you a Warrior of the First Order?"

"I am. This is a very cozy cottage."

The home was warm and inviting, with a stone hearth and furnishings that any fine house would welcome. Nowhere could he see the evidence of her craft. No bottles or jars, or smells in the air.

"This is my home, not my workroom," she smiled. "Please, sit down. I'll brew you some tea, and if you wish, I'll play your game."

"Thank you," he frowned, disturbed that it appeared she could read every thought in his head. "I'm happy to tell you why I'm here, and I didn't mean my question to be any kind of test. I don't doubt your ability one bit. I was just surprised you didn't already know."

Prince Fenderon, the ruler of Zanderone, had told him to speak only the truth and leave nothing out, and as he sat down the warning words whispered through his mind.

"She will know if you are lying or trying to mislead her. You will lose her trust, and that, Darius, will not bode well for the success of your mission."

He watched her move across to the stove and put a kettle on to boil, then open a cupboard, withdraw a jar, and pour a small amount of brown powder into a teapot.

"Do you know Lord Larian and Princess Lizbett?" she asked as she returned and sat opposite him.

"I do."

"Were you at their wedding?"

"No. After the attempt on her father's life the wedding was kept small in number. I was at the reception though. It was held in Prince Fenderon's Palace."

"I know," she said wistfully. "It must have been wonderful."

Angelica enjoyed her life as a witch, but in spite of the many meetings of her coven it was a lonely existence. When she felt the need for a man there were any number of love spells, but they were short-lived, lasting just long enough to enjoy what the man had to offer. It didn't help that if used too often on the same person the spell became less effective, and over time would lose their potency altogether. She could not, and did not, expect to have true love in her life, the kind of love it was rumored Princess Lizbett and Lord Larian shared.

"The Princess and Larian are an interesting couple," Darius remarked.

"They are?" she asked, intrigued by the comment.

"The Princess is strong-minded, and Lord Larian is a Warrior of the First Order, so it was not a likely pairing," he chuckled, "but they certainly seem to have found peace, though I'm not surprised."

"Tell me more," she insisted. *Why can't I see it? Why can't I see the images you have in your head? I know they're in there, I can feel them. Why can't I see them?*

"Perhaps I've already shared too much," he frowned.

"It was rumored that she was very spoilt and difficult until she wedded Lord Larian. How was he able to change her? Being a Princess, and he just a warrior, surely she would have had power over him, not the other way around."

Darius broke into a broad smile.

"Just a warrior," he chuckled. "A Zanderonian warrior, especially a Warrior of the First Order, is not, as you say, just a warrior."

"I must admit, I have met a warrior or two, but they didn't carry your energy," she nodded. "I've heard Lizbett and Larian share a great love. Is that what changed her?"

"Angelica, it is not right for me to gossip about my colleague, or about the Princess, but they are very happy together."

"I wonder what that's like," she mumbled. "Being a witch doesn't allow for such things."

"Perhaps, if the circumstances were right..." he mumbled, not sure what else to say.

Feeling uncomfortable she paused, shifting her mind away from the attempts to learn about the royal couple, and sought the reason for his visit. When it floated into her mind she was greatly relieved, though why she couldn't discern some of his other thoughts, especially those about Lizbett and Larian, was perplexing.

"You are here because you need my help," she declared. "There is trouble in Zanderone, an evil presence, a presence the warriors cannot find or defeat."

"Yes, Angelica, that's exactly why I'm here," he nodded.

"Tell me the details while I pour the tea," she said rising from her chair.

"There is someone, we assume a man, who is causing havoc in Zanderone. He a murderer, killing for sport it seems. Both men and women have fallen victim to his wicked depravity. The people are afraid to leave their homes, merchants won't open their stores for fear of being robbed and killed. Children cannot go outside and play. We don't know how to stop him."

She had poured the tea, and as she brought it back to him, along with some bread smothered in honey she had collected herself, she could feel his angst and see the troubled look in his deep blue eyes, but she felt something else, something unfamiliar, something that made her pulse tick up.

"This tea will strengthen you," she smiled. "You have traveled far to find me. I will make you a proper meal, but the bread and honey can fill the void for the moment. Is your horse in the village?"

"Thank you. The tea has an inviting aroma," he said gratefully. "Yes, I left him in the care of the village stable. My journey was long, and I will need the sleep of Zinyana as the suns fall away tonight."

Zinyana was a deep sleep unique to the warriors. It rejuvenated the body and mind, sinking the subject so deeply into sleep the heart slowed to half its rate; there was no dreaming and no movement.

It was the only time the warrior was vulnerable; he could not leap from his bed, his waking was measured, and he had to straighten his body slowly. Once rising from the state and having eaten, his prowess and strength were restored, and could often function for several days without further rest.

"Do you have somewhere safe for your sleep?" she asked.

"I will seek out an inn at the village."

"Will that give you the protection you need? An inn? I have an extra cot for those who stay here while healing. You are welcome to it. I give you my word I will not bother you."

As his eyes touched hers he could feel her sincerity, and a softness, and a kindness that had not been immediately apparent.

"Thank you, Angelica. I will gratefully accept, but I must ask, will you travel back to Zanderone and help us, can you help us? My Prince is very generous and will pay you handsomely, though I am given to understand you may not be interested in coin. What might we offer you to help us catch this villain?"

"I may be a witch, but I still need to pay for food and items essential to living and for my work, but there may be other forms of payment as well. Yes, Darius, I will help you and your people, and I will think about the cost."

"My Prince and I thank you. It has been a terrible time. When will you be free to travel?"

"In the morning. This evil must be stopped."

"This is wonderful news," he said quietly, then sighing heavily he leaned back, finally feeling that he could catch his breath. "I should collect my horse. Is there a place close where he will be safe?"

"Yes, I have an enclosed area in the back that is quite large. My spell doesn't affect animals, and it offers excellent grazing."

"Thank you. A warrior and his horse don't like to be separated."

"You depend on each other," she remarked.

"We do," he nodded, "and our bond is sacred."

As he sipped his tea and ate the bread with rosemary honey, he could feel himself relax. There had been no guarantee the young witch would agree to travel so far and put herself at risk, Had his request been denied he wasn't sure where else they could turn for help. Lifting his gaze, he found her staring at him.

"Is there a question?"

"No, no question," she replied quietly, *at least, nothing I can ask you. I cannot read you, and I feel a fluttering inside me. I want to lay with you, to enjoy your body, to sit on your manhood, but it is more than that. It is a very pleasant feeling, but it is a worrying one, very worrying indeed.*

CHAPTER TWO

After Darius had finished his tea and bread, Angelica led him down a small hallway to the back of the house, and as he passed by an open door his eye caught sight of a dazzling display of bottles.

"It's my work room, though I prefer to call it my studio," she said turning around.

"I must tell you, it's a bit unsettling how you do that," Darius remarked.

"What?"

"Know what I'm thinking, or feeling, or sense what I'm looking at."

"It's a part of me, like you can go without sleep. Don't worry, I only get bits and pieces," *especially with you, and I'm getting less and less. What's happening? How is it you're blocking my feelers?*

"Would it be all right for me to take a peek?"

"Be my guest," she smiled ushering him in.

Entering the room he gazed in wonder at the cluster of various sized bottles, jars and bowls, none of which were labeled.

"How do you know what everything is, nothing is marked, and how did you learn so much? There must be a hundred jars and bottles in here."

"I am a sixth generation witch."

As he turned around to respond, he found himself captivated by her deep purple eyes and completely forgot what he was about to say.

Am I being mesmerized by this gorgeous creature? Do all men feel like this in her presence, or is it just me?

"I grew up surrounded by far more than what you see here. I am named Angelica because my mother was a deeply bonded with botanicals. I have inherited much of her knowledge and understanding. I instinctively know all that grows around me, and I feel their energy. I do not mark any of my containers because I don't need to, but I have another reason. If someone did manage to break in, how would they know what to steal?"

"Angelica, you are a very impressive young woman," Darius smiled.

"Um, thank you, but I don't consider myself a young woman," she frowned, then abruptly turned away and returned to the hallway.

Bewildered by her statement and sudden change of mood, he fell into step behind her, and was about to ask what she had meant when they reached the back door. It swung itself open, and he found himself stepping outside into a large, lush, fenced pasture.

"This is beautiful," he declared. "River will be very pleased to spend his hours of rest here."

"River? Your horse's name is River?"

"He can move like the rapids, or be as tranquil as an easy flowing waterway," Darius explained.

"The name, it pleases me," she smiled, "and it pleases me that you relate him to one of the elements."

"Most Zanderonian warriors name their horses this way," Darius said. "Lord Larian's horse is called Thunder. He is big, very big, and when he gallops his hoof beats sound just like the growling from the sky."

"You are the first Zanderonian warrior I've met. Perhaps on our journey you could tell me more about your creed."

"I'd be happy to," he nodded, pleased her displeasure appeared to have passed, "but before I leave to bring River back here, there is one thing I must make clear."

"I can feel that you are nervous," she remarked. "Are you going to say something I won't like?"

"Perhaps," he frowned, again finding her talent to read him disconcerting. "Your safety is my first concern. I know you're very self-reliant, which I expected of course, but as long as I am tasked with your protection, it's imperative that you follow my direction."

To his shock she burst out laughing.

"You protect me? You think you need to protect me?"

"Of course," he replied. "Why you find this amusing?"

"Darius, if there is a need for protection, it will be me protecting you!"

"Angelica, you may be a witch," he shot back, "and I have been told you are an exceptional witch, but if we should be intercepted by robbers, or if we find ourselves confronting the devil man who is terrifying the people of Zanderone, my sword and my fighting skills will see us safe. You must remain behind me, or if I have placed you somewhere to keep you out of harm's way, you must stay there. You must do as I tell you. There is no argument here. Do I make myself clear?"

He had grown taller as he'd delivered his lecture, his voice had deepened, and a serious glint had crossed his eye.

"Yes, Darius, you made yourself clear," she said softly, *and how easy you are to convince. All I said was yes, in a sweet, feminine way, and you completely believed me. Tsk, tsk. You forget I am a witch, not one of those giggly young women you compared me to.*

"Oh, well, good then," he coughed, finding her quick capitulation surprising. "I'll be on my way. It won't take me long to fetch River and ride him back."

"I'll start some dinner."

"This spell of yours that protects your house," he said as they ambled through her garden to the front gate, "does it also mean someone can't wander out of our house once they're inside?"

"Most definitely," she nodded, "but there is a sack of specially blended herbs I can provide that will allow it."

"Interesting. Should I have that sack so when I return-"

"I will know when you are back," she interrupted smiling up at him, "and I will bring you in with your horse."

"Of course you will know when I'm back," he sighed.

"I'm sorry if my talents annoy you," she said raising her eyebrows. "I am a witch. It is just in me."

They had reached the front gate, and he noticed groupings of flowers scattered across the front lawn surrounded by circles of white and ebony stones.

"That's very attractive," he remarked.

"Thank you."

"Like you."

The words had spilled out before he'd even realized they'd formed in his head.

"I, uh, am I?" she stuttered.

Staring down at her, he saw her pale complexion begin to turn pink.

"Surely you must know that," he said kindly. "You are a very lovely young woman."

"I told you, I'm not a young woman," she snapped the sweetness suddenly evaporating.

"I'm sorry," he said quickly, "I meant no insult."

"You'd best go and fetch your horse," she quipped. "You need to step outside the gate."

"I really am sorry, it was a compliment," he continued as he moved outside of her fence.

"Young women are foolish, indolent, stupid creatures," she exclaimed, "and I do not wish to be compared to them."

"Then you are a lovely young witch," he said, "I hope that's correct, because you are, you are lovely."

"I, uh, thank you," she replied looking away, then hurried back to her cottage.

Staring after her, he watched her slip inside and close her door.

How very odd. So confident, so smart, but she just fell apart. This will be an interesting journey.

Breaking into a jog he headed for the village, the image of the beguiling young witch lodged in his mind's eye.

Closing the door Angelica moved quickly to her stove. Dropping some pink powder into a cup, she poured in some hot water, then added a teaspoon of thick syrup from a jar. Swirling the mixture with a spoon she watched the powder dissolve, then swallowed the sweet, soothing drink in two gulps.

What is wrong with me? When his eyes touch mine I feel so strange, and when he said those kind words my whole body went hot. He thinks I'm lovely? I felt no falsehood when he said it, but I've never thought I was lovely. Men don't see me as lovely, men just see a witch...don't they?

Moving to her bedroom she stood before her tall oval mirror and stared at her reflection.

"I am as I have always been," she muttered. "I am not unattractive, but lovely?"

Looking across at her grey cat curled up on the bed, she laid down next to him and stroked his soft fur.

"What do you think, Moon? Do you think I'm lovely?"

Stretching, the cat opened his yellow eyes and stared up at her.

"My precious puss, you must take care of things around here for several passes of the suns. Will you do that?"

The cat meowed a few times, then rubbed himself against her.

"I'll be leaving tomorrow morning. You know what to do, but I must tell you, Moon, I am feeling the need. It has been a while, but it's that warrior, Darius, he has filled me with it. I think I'll feel better if I rub it away."

Laying on her back, Angelica spread her legs and placed her fingers against her sex. As a rule, Angelica didn't wear any underthings, and as she closed her eyes and touched herself the warm sensations began.

"Oh, yes," she muttered, "I do feel the need, very much."

She imagined the magnificent warrior holding her in his powerful arms, then his hands clutching the cheeks of her bottom as he pulled her against his body. The pictures were so clear, the feel of his member rubbing against her almost real, and the smell of him, ooh, the smell of him. She'd been drawn to his scent even before he'd stepped from the shadows, and standing near him she'd found it as delicious as the aroma of her triple-berry, mulled wine with the shaved cinnamon bark.

What would you do if you had me? Would you hold me down, or would you want me to straddle you? I've heard rumors about the Zanderonian warriors and their lovemaking skill. I wonder if they're true.

Her moment was upon her, and as she surrendered to the tantalizing, shuddering, tingling release, she sent him a message.

I want you. I want your hands to explore me, your lips to kiss me, and your cock to slide inside me. Think upon it, Darius, think upon it and imagine it. Think how you wish to sweep me into your warrior's hold and worship my body, then return and make it happen.

The image of the beautiful witch had stayed with Darius, and his curiosity had been percolating. He had paid the stable manager, chatted for a moment, and was riding back towards the forest when Angelica's image sharpened, and he found he had a burning desire to kiss her.

"Hmm, to kiss a witch," he muttered. "Is there a danger there? What do you think, River? She is certainly kissable."

The need lingered, and as the seconds passed became even more fervent.

"What is this?" he murmured. "It's like a fever, like nothing I've felt before. Hmm, I think this might be the work of a wicked little witch. If it is, you have met your match in me, young lady."

Closing his eyes he fought back, pushing away her insistent call and resurrecting his focus on his mission.

From all the elite Warriors of the First Order, the Prince had selected him, and it was a great honor. He was instructed to find Angelica, to win her agreement to help, then return her safely to Zanderone. In spite of her youth she was reputed to be cunning, clever and exceptionally skilled, and as he wound his way through the trees, the fever having left him, Darius couldn't help but smile.

CHAPTER THREE

"**H**e's near," Angelica mumbled.

She was standing at her stove stirring the simmering rabbit stew. Knowing he would soon envelop her in his arms and carry her to her bed, she hurried to back to her bedroom to run a comb through her hair and dab pomegranate juice on her lips. It would redden them and give a sweet tartiness to the flavor of her kiss. Except for the time when she'd felt drawn to a sorcerer's son and had wanted to please his scrutinizing eye, she'd not particularly cared about her appearance.

I don't know why Darius is affecting me this way, and it is troubling, but I like this feeling. There is a thrill in my veins. I've not felt such a thrill before. I must have him in my arms, I must.

It had been a simple spell, the incantation hadn't even rhymed, nor had she used the phrase, *so I ask it, so it shall be,* thinking it unnecessary. He was a man, he was fallible in such things. Drawing him into her bed was easy.

"Oh! He's here," she muttered, and moving quickly through the house and out the front door, she reached the gate just as he appeared.

"What a beautiful horse!" she exclaimed. "Follow me. We can bring him in through the back gate of the pasture."

As she neared, River snorted and dropped his head against her chest.

"Ah, yes, sweet, River, you are a noble steed."

"He likes you," Darius chuckled. "I don't think I've ever seen him do that before."

"I am in touch with him," she smiled as she stroked his head. "He is happy to be away from the stable. He doesn't like to be away from you. He worries."

"Yes, I believe I mentioned that," Darius remarked.

"You think I am trying to dupe you?" she asked, her deep purple eyes blazing up at him.

"Not at all," he replied. "Must you be so defensive?"

"I just, uh, thought you were doubting me," she said dropping her gaze back down. "Uh, no, I wasn't doubting you," Darius frowned, *and if you can read my thoughts you should have known that.*

"The man at the stables tried to feed him grain he didn't like," she remarked.

"Yes, the barn manager mentioned that," Darius muttered. *This is very confusing. One minute she can read me, the next minute she can't, unless, did she get that from River? No, that's not possible.*

"Follow me, River. I think your Master has much to learn about the talents of this witch."

"Apparently," he muttered.

As River walked along beside her with no coaxing from him, Darius was in awe. It was one thing to feel connected to an animal, but so quickly and so deeply?

When they neared the gate, Darius didn't need to pull on his reins. When Angelica, stopped, so did River. Dismounting, he unbuckled the girth, gently sliding the saddle off the horse's back, then led him forward into the pasture.

"I'm so pleased you have this paddock," he smiled as he removed the bridle. "River needs this thick, green grass. It's nourishing for both his body and his soul."

"It is how nature intends for a horse to eat," she nodded. "I have already filled a water barrel for him, so if you bring that saddle, you can keep it safe in the tool shed in the garden."

"Thank you, Angelica,"

With her hand looped around his elbow, he carried it around the side of the house and placed it in the small shed.

"Everything is so neatly arranged," he remarked as he studied the various tools carefully laid out.

"I try to keep everything organized," she smiled. "Now we can relax. The suns are dropping from the sky, but we will be warm by my fire," *and your body will soon be on top of mine, and there is nothing that can keep me warmer than that.*

Taking his hand she walked him back to the cottage, and once inside she stared up at him expectantly.

"Is there a basin where I can wash my hands?" he asked.

"Uh, yes, at my sink near the stove," she replied. *Why aren't you kissing me? You should be holding me and kissing me right now.*

"Whatever you're cooking smells delicious," he declared as he moved past her.

"I hope you enjoy it," she said completely puzzled by his cavalier attitude.

Maybe he wants to be clean before he holds me. Yes, that must be it, he wants to be clean.

"If you would like a full tub I have one. I like to soak in water frequently."

"Perhaps later," he replied taking a cloth from the counter and wiping his hands dry. "You're looking at me strangely. Is there something on your mind?"

"No, no," she lied, "nothing at all. Please, sit down at the table and I'll pour you some of my mulberry wine." *Why has the charm spell not worked, and why don't I know what you're thinking?*

"Angelica," he said moving towards her, "would you come and rest on the couch with me for a moment."

"Of course," she smiled. *Finally, this is it. He just wanted to be somewhere comfortable. Of course!*

As she followed him across the kitchen into the living area, her heart began to beat with a hard, pulsing rhythm, and when he sat down and extended his hand she felt odd, almost nervous. Angelica was rarely nervous.

"I am a Warrior of the First Order," he began. "Do you know what that means?"

"It means you are very skilled," she replied. "One of the elite, one of the best warriors in Zanderone, like Lord Larian."

"Yes, it does mean that, but it also means you are not the only one who has highly tuned senses."

"Uh, what are you saying?" she frowned.

"You have lied to me. If we are to journey together and fight this evil man when we reach Zanderone, we cannot have falsehoods between us. We must be able to trust each other completely."

Never had Angelica felt her skin flush as it did. A hot burn crossed her cheeks, and as his blue eyes penetrated hers she felt compelled to drop her gaze.

"Tell me, what's on your mind," Darius asked, "and why did you say there wasn't when I asked?"

"I was, uh, upset that I couldn't bring you this special cheese that I-"

"Oh, dear," he interrupted.

"What?" she asked still studying the floor.

"Now you have told me two lies," he sighed. "Do you know what that means?"

Lifting her gaze she stared back at him, desperately trying to read the images in his head.

"No," she mumbled.

"If we are to work as a team you must know such lies will not be tolerated, not for a moment. I'm afraid I must punish you. You must be subject to my discipline,"

"Punishment? Discipline?" she frowned. "I am the one that punishes, I am the one that hands out justice."

"Not this time, Angelica, not if you wish to keep your promise to help the people of Zanderone."

"This is impossible," she exclaimed jumping to her feet.

"Such a pity," he sighed. "In that case, I would be grateful of the meal you have offered, and the cot in which I can rest in Zinyana. River and I will leave in the morning and take the bad news back to my Prince."

"No! No," she shouted. "I do want to help, I do. I want to travel with you and I want to-"

"Then you must accept that you are subject to my rule and to my discipline," he said calmly.

"I have, uh, never been under someone's rule," she stammered, "except the rules of my Coven."

"The choice is yours."

"This is…this is…not doable," she sputtered.

"Then, as I said, I will leave in the morning."

She stared at him, amazed by his strong will and deep calm.

I want to do this. I want to travel with him. This is so frustrating. What should I do?

"Um, what do you mean by punishment," she finally asked, "what will you do to me?"

"That depends," he replied. "For lying, I shall simply warm your bottom. I suspect that will be enough to keep you truthful. Blatant disobedience could mean other forms of punishment, but I will never cause you such discomfort that you will hate me. You might for a moment, I suppose, but not for long."

Angelica hadn't heard anything he'd said past the three words, *warm your bottom.*

"What do you mean, warm my bottom?" she breathed.

"Spank you," he said simply.

"Spank me?"

"Yes, spank you," he repeated, "while you are lying over my lap."

The hot burn she'd initially felt was now permeating every part of her, and the need between her legs she'd so efficiently dispatched, had returned with a rush of warm moisture.

"I cannot," she stammered.

"Again I am saddened," he frowned. "I believe I will go and check on River."

An unexpected wave of his disappointment washed over her, and in spite of her muddled state, her instinct told her she was making a mistake, a big one.

"Wait!" she said putting her hand on his arm. "I, uh, I accept, and I will tell you the truth."

"Are you sure?"

"Yes, yes, I am sure," she fervently nodded, "I would only ask that you not spank me too hard. I've never had a hand strike me before."

"I will spank you as hard as I believe I should," he replied soberly. "Sit back down and tell me what was bothering you, what is still bothering you."

"This is difficult," she mumbled perching on the edge of the couch.

"Just say it. In my younger years, when I was faced with a similar situation," he said tenderly, "rarely were things as grave as I feared."

"I hope you're right," she sighed. "I expected you to, uh, hug me when you returned from the village."

"You did? Why was that?"

"Because I, uh…"

As he'd strongly suspected, his burning desire to kiss her as he'd been riding through the forest was because she had cast some kind of spell.

"Angelica, have you been a mischievous witch?" he asked sternly. "Tell me the truth. Did you try to put a spell on me, not to hug you, but to kiss you?"

"Ooh, yes, yes, I did," she confessed dropping her head into her hands.

"So, the truth comes out. What a naughty witch. I might very well kiss you, but if I do, it will be my wish. Why would you want a man to kiss you because you have put a spell on him? Surely you would want a man to kiss you because he desires you."

"I don't know what to say," she bleated. "If I see a man I like, I have to cast a spell. What man wants to kiss a witch? Men don't like witches, they only fear us."

"I certainly don't fear you," he declared, "and you do need to be punished. Lay yourself over my lap immediately."

She didn't anticipate the power behind his command, and feeling as if she was suddenly under some kind of spell herself, she slowly stretched herself across thick, muscled thighs.

"I can't believe I'm doing this," she groaned. "Who would dare spank a witch, especially me?"

"Are you saying I should fear your spells?"

"Well, kind of," she muttered.

"You tried one, and considering you're over my knee about to be spanked I'd say it didn't work very well."

"It wasn't a very strong spell," she quipped, wriggling as she tried to get comfortable.

Her comment made him chuckle, and he smoothed his wide hand across her upturned bottom.

"Why are you laughing?" she demanded.

"A Zanderonian warrior, especially a Warrior of the First Order, has been trained to deal with many things, but we are still just men, yes, and while you are a witch, you are still just a woman."

"I suppose," she bleated.

"You have talent, and now, my mischievous little witch, you have met a man who also has talent, perhaps more than you, and that man is going to spank your very deserving bottom."

Raising his hand, he sent it flying down with a strong swat, followed immediately by a second and a third. Her shrill yelp bounced off the walls, and as he started on her opposite cheek, Moon, her cat, ran into the room. Darius glared at him, and raising his finger in the air he pointed to the door.

"Out!"

Moon didn't wait for a second command, and quickly pranced away.

"How did you do that?" she mewled. "He only listens to me."

"As I just told you," he said fondling her cheeks and delighting in their plumpness, "I have been trained in many things."

He resumed his work, swatting her backside with a flurry of hard smacks.

"Some ground rules," he declared as he continued. "You will not attempt to cast any further spells on me. Do you promise?"

"OW! Yes, I promise!"

"You will not lie to me."

"OW, OW, No! I won't, I promise."

"You will do as I say, especially when we're facing danger."

"Yes, yes, I will. I'll do as I'm told."

"Three more very hard on each cheek to underscore your three promises," he decreed, "but with this dress up."

"NOOO!"

Ignoring her wailing plea he slipped the thin gown up her legs, and was shocked to find her naked, the pink stain of his hand glowing up at him.

"What is this? No undergarments?"

"I don't wear them, not usually," she mewled.

Not sure how to respond, he landed his six hard slaps, delivering them slowly, waiting between each, allowing their sting to permeate.

"Do we have a clear understanding?" he asked as he gently caressed her seared skin.

"Yes, yes, we do," she whimpered.

"Good. You can expect more of the same if you break any of those promises, but the spanking will be harder, and perhaps with an implement, not just my hand."

"I won't break them," she whimpered, "I swear."

"I hope not," he sighed continuing to rub away the sting. "Now I'm going to ask you something and I expect the truth. You can read my thoughts, but not all the time. Is that right?"

"I can sense your feelings, I can sense if you are sincere, but I can only read your thoughts sometimes, and I can't see any of your pictures."

"Thank you, Angelica, now get up, sit down and face me."

Slowly rising, rubbing her hot, stinging cheeks, she paused for a moment before gingerly sitting down.

"Now," he said softly, cupping her chin, "now I will kiss you."

CHAPTER FOUR

H is free hand clutched the hair at the back of her head, and as he smoothed his lips over hers, a hot tingling rippled down her spine. His lips were startlingly soft, and though he pressed them gently, and moved them with a tender, comforting kindness, she could sense his power, and it sent a pulsing need through her sex.

"There," he said pulling back, "there is your kiss. It was given because I chose to offer it, because I wanted to, because I find you lovely."

"Why do you find me lovely?" she whispered breathlessly.

"First, you will thank me."

"Thank you for kissing me," she sighed wishing she could lean her head into the hollow of his shoulder.

"What else?" he insisted, his hand still gripping her hair.

"I don't, uh…

"Think about it. You're a smart young witch."

"Oh, for spanking me? You want me to thank you for spanking me?"

"Of course. If I didn't care about you and if I didn't want you to travel with me, I wouldn't have bothered. Don't you see that?"

"I suppose," she mumbled, "yes, I think perhaps I do. Thank you, Darius, for spanking me. Saying that felt weird."

"That's because, you naughty witch, paying for your sins is foreign to you."

"I, uh, I don't know what to say. Please will you let my hair go?"

"No, I haven't finished with you yet. You asked me why you're lovely. Do you still want to know?"

"I do, yes, definitely," *and I wish my pulse would stop racing, and I wish he would hold me, and move his large hands over my body.*

"Your lips are so wonderfully red, and it's not just the stain of the fruits you use," he smiled.

Gazing at her, he could feel her hunger and see the longing in her deep purple eyes, and though he ached to take her he was hesitant. While he knew her yearning was mostly physical, his instinct told him there could be more. He had no wish to break her heart, and he couldn't deny there was something stirring to life in his.

"Your eyes," he continued, "they sparkle like the stars. Your skin is almost as white as the first snow, yet it blushes so beautifully. The body beneath this dress is full and sensitive, and in spite of being a witch you carry a passionate soul. Those are some of the reasons I think you're lovely."

Before she could answer he kissed her again, but this time with fervor, and bringing his free hand to her breasts he held each in turn, molding them in his broad hand.

"Oh, Darius, please will you lay with me, please," she begged, her voice a whispered breath as he slipped his mouth to her neck.

"No, Angelica, not yet, not quite yet."

"Why not?" she bleated.

"Because I said so," he purred into her ear, "and you will learn to listen. You're used to having things your own way, and that is something I intend to change."

"It's not fair," she grumbled.

"You sound like a spoiled child," he chuckled. "Go and put dinner on the table before I spank you again."

"I like it here, sitting next to you like this," she mumbled. "I'd like it even more if I was curled up in your lap."

"If you are a good witch and you behave yourself, you might find yourself there one day."

"It is strange that you don't fear me. All the men I've met have feared me."

"You haven't met a Zanderonian warrior," he smiled, and releasing her hair he took her hand, pulled her to her feet and swatted her sharply.

"OUCH," she yelped, then impulsively threw her arms around his neck.

"I see," he grinned holding her tightly. "If you don't get what you want, you just take it."

"I need a hug," she said sinking into him. *This is very strange. He is just a man, but he is more than a man, and my body is on fire. There is so much wetness between my legs and I want him, I want him badly.*

"That's enough," he said firmly, gently pulling her arms down. "It's obvious you also lack self-discipline, which surprises me. I would think you would have to control certain urges to be a witch. How do you not curse people, or put spells on those who have done you wrong?"

"How do you know I don't?" she replied gazing up at him.

"I think this is a conversation for another time, and we will be able to talk as we travel. Now, please, are you going to feed this hungry warrior, or is he going to jump on his horse and ride into the village?"

"I shall feed you," she said all smiles again. "It's ready."

Taking his hand she led him into the kitchen, and as he settled at the fine wooden table with the straight-backed chairs, he enjoyed the sight of her pottering around. Pulling out the bread that had been warming in the oven, she broke it into chunks and dropped them into deep bowls, then ladled in the thick stew

"It smells delicious," he grinned as she set one of the bowls in front of him. "Thank you."

"I'll get you some mulberry wine. It's not very strong, but it is very tasty."

Humming happily, she pulled a pitcher from a cupboard, splashed the deep purple liquid into pewter goblets and placed them on the table.

"I had a sense I'd be receiving a visitor," she said sitting opposite him, "so I prepared all this after I finished my morning meal."

"My goodness, this is the best stew I've ever had," he exclaimed. "You are an exceptional cook."

"There are herbs that like to be married and must be paired, there are others that want to lurk in the background, and then there are those that demand center stage. If you understand herbs, you understand how to flavor food properly," she announced.

"You could teach the Palace cooks a thing or two," he said as he continued to devour the meal. "Perhaps, after we have finished our work in Zanderone, you could talk to the workers in the kitchen and share some of your knowledge."

"Only if I'm welcome," she replied. "Most people don't like a witch for company."

"They don't need to know you're a witch. You could be introduced as a friend of mine. A friend who is an excellent cook."

"Hmmm, maybe, if the Prince would like me to," she nodded, "and speaking of the Prince, I know what I want as payment."

"What's that?" he asked lifting a copious mouthful of the rich gravy with a piece of soaked bread.

"I do want coin, but it doesn't have to be excessive. Perhaps a month's salary of a Warrior of the First Order, or double the reward of the capture of someone less important. Whatever the Prince feels is right."

"That is generous of you, Angelica, and I know he will be in return. What else?"

"I want to meet Princess Lizbett and Lord Larian. I want to spend time with them, have dinner, perhaps even stay overnight at their house. I want to see how they are together, and have private words with Princess Lizbett."

"That's interesting. Why?"

"I just do," she said casting her eyes down.

"I need a bit more than that," he said firmly.

"Very well," she sighed, "if you insist. I've never been around a couple like that, a couple that everyone talks about as being so in love and so happy. I want to see it, I want sense how it feels."

"No mischief?"

"No," she promised. "I am very curious about this depth of love between a man and a woman. How did it change her? Why did it change her? Only talking to her privately and being in their presence can my questions be answered."

"I can understand that," he nodded. "You'll be very pleased to know that Larian will be my partner in the hunt for this killer, so we will be staying at his house when we first arrive. I live very close by, but the three of us together overnight will give us a chance to become better acquainted. We'll leave in the morning to ride into the city where we will be welcomed as guests at Prince Fenderon's Palace."

"We'll be staying with Princess Lizbett and Lord Larian, and then at the Palace?" she asked excitedly.

"We will. Anything else?"

"I'm just so thrilled at the news I can hardly think. Um, there may be some varieties of plants and shrubs in Zanderone I don't have here. If there are, I would like seedlings to bring back with me. I enjoy meeting new botanicals."

"That's easy," he nodded.

"There is one last thing," she said quietly.

"I'm listening."

"I want your promise that you will visit me after I return here, and I mean visit me often. I like being around you. I am enjoying the company of a man who is, um, different."

"I promise. I would like to, very much, especially if you feed me like this," he smiled.

"Then we shall be leaving in the morning," she smiled back at him, "and I have some special pudding. I don't know what to call it, but it's very good."

"I have no doubt," he chuckled.

"I didn't know it would be a Zanderonian warrior visiting, but my instinct told me to make it, and now I know why. I think I'll call it, Lavender Dream, because lavender is an excellent sleep aid, not that you need it with Zinyana."

"I can't wait to try it," he said eagerly.

Rising from the table she collected the dishes, placed them on the counter, then pulling a square tin from a cabinet next to the oven, she placed it in the center of the table and offered him a spoon.

"I eat it straight from the pan," she giggled. "I don't know why, but it tastes better that way."

Sinking the spoon into the soft, creamy mixture, he let it melt against his tongue, then rolled his eyes.

"What is in this?" he asked. *I want to smooth it over your luscious breasts and tongue it off, and I really hope you didn't just read that thought.*

"Dried lavender, goat cheese, cream, honey, and a tiny bit of blueberry and vanilla essence," *and I'm sensing something, something warm from you, something you want from me, or is it something you want to do to me?*

After slowly spooning mouthful after mouthful of the delicious dessert, he leaned back in his chair and yawned.

"It is time. I must rest in Zinyana," he declared.

"I made your cot ready when you went into the village," she said. "Please come with me."

"Do you know the rules?" he asked as she led him down a short passageway. "Do not disturb me unless it's an emergency, and do not lay against me."

"I understand," she replied opening a door. "Here you are."

Moving past her, he raised his eyes in surprise. It was much more than a cot. A decent sized bed covered in thick coverlets and two puffy pillows sat in the center of the room, a modest nightstand next to it. A small potbellied stove was in the corner, and a table with a chair sat under a paned window that overlooked the paddock.

"This is much more than I expected," he declared as he peered out at his horse happily grazing in the lush grass. "I shall rest very well here, very well indeed."

"I hope so. If you need anything, my room is on the other side of the kitchen next to my workroom. There is an outhouse just through there," she said pointing to a door that would take him outside. "The key rests in the lock, so you can bolt it if you think it's necessary, but no-one will be able to reach the cottage without me."

"This is excellent indeed," he nodded, then yawning again he dropped on to the bed. "You must leave me now."

"Rest well. I'll have the morning meal waiting whenever you wander into the kitchen."

He saw a soft smile in her eyes, and as she closed the door he began to undress, pulling off his boots, then stripping off his clothes.

Slipping under the bedcovers he let out a heavy sigh, and gazing across at the window he could see the light from the two suns had faded, and darkness was creeping across the sky. Try as he might, he could not deny the need in his cock. She had brought the ache to life, and pushing back the coverlets he wrapped his fingers around himself.

Recalling the plump roundness of her bottom as he exacted his discipline, then the feel of her luscious breasts in his hand, he surrendered to the growing climax. It was rapidly building, and with a desire to release quickly, he imagined her completely naked kneeling in front of him, her eyes lowered and her palms resting on his thighs, the position of supplication. She was such a naughty, willful witch, picturing her in the ultimate position of respect and surrender was all he needed. His cock exploded across his hand, and gritting his teeth to stifle his groans, he sank joyfully into the hot prickles cascading through his limbs.

As the moment passed, he reached for his shirt and wiped himself clean, then sank back into the mattress. The bed was supremely soft, almost too soft, but as he felt his body sink into Zinyana he was grateful for its forgiveness, and closing his eyes he allowed his mind to drift.

She is not to be trusted. You have her under control for the moment, but only for the moment. You were told she is unpredictable, and she has shown she is mischievous. Be careful, don't let your guard down, and take nothing for granted.

In her workroom, Angelica was humming happily, Moon sitting on her table as she blended various herbs, grinding them with her pestle and mortar then pouring them into separate leather sacks.

"He thinks he's in total control," she giggled. "It is best I allow him to believe that. I do want to be with him, I do want to travel with him and deal with the evil that is hurting the people of Zanderone, but he has no idea about me, does he, Moon?"

The yellow-eyed, silver cat had been laying down, contentedly purring, but as she had spoken, he had meowed, and standing up and stretching, he moved closer to her.

"I am still bewildered though, sweet cat," she continued taking a moment to scratch his head. "I am so drawn to him, and my bottom is sore, but I like it. Why would I like such a thing? I need to speak to Aunt Namia. It's only a short distance from the main road on the way to Zanderone. He won't mind if I need to make a quick stop, in fact, I'll make sure he won't, isn't that right, Moon? The only question is, how can I do that without lying to him?"

Rubbing against her hand, he lifted his head and stared her.

"That is an excellent suggestion," she giggled. "Why didn't I think of it? You are a very clever cat," and picking up one of the sacks, she emptied out its contents.

CHAPTER FIVE

Darius was waking. He could feel the life return to his muscles, the gentle uptick of his heart, and the tingling pins and needles at the tips of his fingers and his toes. The heaviness in his eyelids began to lift, and he slowly moved his limbs. Stretching carefully, he opened his eyes and gradually moved his head to gaze out the window. There was light, but the suns were low; he had woken at precisely the right time.

Sitting up he raised his arms above his head and yawned, then carefully rising to his feet he wandered to the window to check on River. What he saw took his breath away.

Standing outside the pasture fence was a stunningly beautiful, pure white horse with a thick, wavy mane and tail.

"If I didn't know better I'd say you were a unicorn that lost its horn," he muttered.

The horse was slightly smaller than River, and was standing peacefully, as if waiting. River was grazing, but lifted his head every few seconds to look across at his ivory visitor.

"My goodness, what next?" Darius mumbled pulling on his clothes.

Opening the bedroom door he smelled a delicious aroma wafting from the kitchen, and as he ambled down the short hallway he could hear Angelica humming. It made him smile, and he paused to listen.

"Good morning," she called.

"Good morning," he called back. *Of course you knew I was here.* "I just saw a white horse outside the paddock," he remarked entering the kitchen.

"That's Spirit," she smiled as she placed some dishes on the table.

"Spirit?"

"My mare."

"I don't understand. Did she escape?"

"Spirit is not kept locked up. She doesn't need to be. She always comes when I call, and if she wants to graze the paddock is there for her. I make sure it's always full and lush."

"How extraordinary," he murmured. "I've never heard of such a thing."

"This does not surprise me," she smiled. "Would you like tea, or juice, or-"

"Hot tea, I think," he said sitting down. "Are you planning to ride her when we leave?"

"Of course," she laughed bringing him a steaming mug. "Why do you think I called her home?"

"I just assumed you'd be riding with me."

"No, that wouldn't be very wise. If anything happened to you or River, I'd be stranded. I'll feel much safer riding Spirit."

"I can understand your point," he mumbled. *It just never occurred to me that you'd have a horse and want to ride all the way to Zanderone.* "I have a change of clothing, and if possible I'd like to use that tub of yours before we leave."

"I have already started to fill it," she smiled. "It has one of those new wheels that lets the water flow in."

"You know everything I want before I want it," he said shaking his head. "I have to admit it's a bit unnerving, and how is it you have a water wheel? They're only found in the finest of homes."

"It was payment for some help I gave a nobleman," she replied setting plates of various foods in front of him. "The

34

water's been filling for a while. I'd better check and make sure it's not going to run over the sides."

Staring after her as she left the kitchen, he sipped his tea, a bemused frown crossing his brow.

Will the surprises never end? A horse that is never behind a fence or tethered, a tub with water wheel, a garden I cannot pass unless she is at my side. If I wasn't seeing all this with my own eyes I'm not sure I'd believe it, and she's a mere slip of a girl. My confidence that she can help me fight this evil at home is growing. I wonder what tricks she'll have up her sleeve for that.

Picking up his spoon he began to eat, and was again almost overcome by the flavors that fell against his tongue.

What a catch you will be for some lucky fellow. You are lovely to look at, your food is better than any I've tasted, and you have such a twinkle in those deep purple eyes. What a shame men are afraid of you.

"How is your morning meal?" she asked as she stepped back in the room.

"Excellent, truly excellent. Will you be ready to leave after I soak and change my clothes?"

"Yes, I have everything prepared," she nodded. "I don't need much, and I have already packed us some food so we will be able to stop and eat when we feel like it."

"I believe you will be an excellent traveling companion," he smiled.

"Thank you. I must ask you about this devil in your realm. Do you have anything he may have worn or touched?"

"My goodness, it completely slipped my mind," he exclaimed dropping his spoon. "Did you know that I had something, or-"

"Sometimes I know things I don't know," she interrupted. "That sounds strange. What I mean is, I didn't know you had something, I didn't even feel it, but the question came to me anyway."

"Fascinating," he sighed. "I do have an object. It was found near his last victim, and her family said they'd never seen it

35

before so we assumed it must have been his. It's in my saddle bag with my change of clothes."

"You keep eating. I'll fetch the bag for you."

Angelica stepped out into the early morning and gazed at the sky. There was a hint of rain in the air, but it was too far away to be of concern, and she could feel that their first day of travel would be pleasantly warm. Closing her eyes she reached her hands to the heavens.

Sun of the East, protect our journey
Light our path and keep us warm
Sun of the West, protect our journey
If there is danger, I ask that you warn
Sun of the East, Sun of the West
I call upon help from both of ye,
So I ask it, so it shall be.

Slowly opening her eyes she let out a breath, then opened her garden shed to collect his saddle bag. Running her fingers over the leather of his saddle a small smile curled the edges of her lips. She could see him galloping through the open plains, she could sense his deep loyalty and huge heart, but then a surprising heaviness filled her. Placing both hands on the seat she leaned into it, searching for the cause, but it remained a furtive shadow.

This is so odd. Again I am stymied, unable to see through his impenetrable veil. Could a Zanderonian warrior simply possesses this shroud of protection? Perhaps that's it. Perhaps they develop this through their years of training.

Finding some comfort in the theory, she lifted the saddle bag and carried it inside, and walking into the kitchen she found Darius had finished his meal and his tea mug was empty.

"Here you are," she smiled as she handed it to him. "I'll get you more tea."

"Thank you, Angelica, and what is in that tea?"

"Black tea leaves ground with cinnamon, a tiny amount of skin from an orange, and a clove."

"I could drink it all day," he grinned, "and no doubt it is only one of many brews."

"Yes, only one," she nodded taking his mug and pouring him some more.

"This is what was found," he said retrieving a rounded piece of metal from his saddle bag and placing it on the table. "It looks like some kind of armband, but we can't be sure. I think I'll take this tea and sip it while I soak. By the time I finish I will have returned to full strength and we can leave."

"Let me show you to the anteroom," she smiled.

"It's just by your workroom isn't? I'm sure I can find it," he said rising from his chair, and taking his mug and saddle bag he headed towards the passageway.

Sitting down, Angelica lifted the silver band from the table, and holding it in her hands she closed her eyes.

Owner of this band
I know you walk afar
Owner of this band
Show me who you are
Owner of this band
Submit your thoughts to me
Owner of this band
I demand you let it be.

The revelation began with a dark swirling mist, and a cold shiver shuddered through her body. It wasn't pleasant, the energy was pained and angry, but she stayed with it, waiting for the mist to clear.

A man appeared, and though he wasn't old he appeared grizzled and aged. His eyes were bulbous and icy grey, his heart cold, and so filled with hatred as to barely be alive. His hair fell long and straggly, and with great concentration she pulled back to view the rest of him. A tall, thin body sat behind loose clothing. It was void of muscle or fat, but she sensed the man moved fast, lightening fast. He could disappear into shadow, and was so light on his feet as to be silent.

A jolt broke her from her trance, and dropping the object she sighed deeply, then hastily moved to her stove to make herself a potion that would expel any dark energy she may have absorbed.

When Darius returned in fresh clothes and ready to head out, he found her sitting at the table waiting for him, her hands clasped around her mug, her cat curled up in front of her.

"What's wrong?" he asked seeing the cloud in her eyes.

"Please sit down, Darius," she said somberly.

"This feels ominous," he said settling opposite her.

"The owner of this band is filled with intense hatred for Zanderone and its people. I cannot say if it was left deliberately as a message, or if it fell from him. He is very thin, so he would not have been wearing it, but it's possible he carries it with him and it was accidentally dropped."

"You know this person is a man?"

"Yes, I was able to conjure his image. As I mentioned he's thin. He looks much older than he is, he has long, stringy hair and wears loose clothing. He moves in the shadows, and he's quick and strong and kills effortlessly"

"That's amazing," he breathed.

"I feel he has a purpose, though I also feel these are revenge killings. We live in peaceful times. We have not seen wars for some time. Can you think of where-"

"I know what this is," he interrupted, a deep frown crossing his brow.

"I can feel your deep worry," she said softly. "Please, you must tell me."

"Yes, I must. It was back many passes of the moons, before I was a Warrior of the First Order. There was a group unknown to us that settled themselves on the outskirts of the Kingdom. The Prince gave his permission on the condition they stay within certain boundaries. It wasn't long before the local farmers noticed their livestock was disappearing, so they came to the

Palace and stated their case. The Prince sent out some warriors to talk with the settlers. I was one of those warriors."

"These people sound like the marauders," Angelica remarked, "the people who live in the barren lands. Didn't they turn over the traitors that attempted to kill the King of Verdana, Lizbett's father?"

"They did, but unfortunately these settlers were not marauders. There were only six of us, but a single Zanderonian warrior is able to defend against many men. We entered their camp, and my Commander asked to speak to the leader. Without warning we were set upon. Men and women attacked us with weapons we'd never seen before, like round swirling knives that sailed through the air. Had it not been for our quick reactions we might well have lost our lives. We had to defend ourselves, and most of the attackers were slain. We are not killers, and we tried our best to corral them, to tether them, to injure them just enough to stop the fighting, but they were like wild animals. There was no stopping them. It was obvious they would to fight to the death. Before we left the Commander ordered those remaining to leave the realm immediately. Could this killer in Zanderone be a son of those people? From what you described, I believe this is the case."

"Ah, yes, it feels right," she nodded. "What a terrible story. I am feeling something about them. Something...odd. Do you know where from where they hail?"

"No, we never did find out. They were strange looking. Tall, and thin, with sharp chins and huge eyes. Their camp was by a river, and their skin was almost the color of the rocks."

"I sense they came from far away," Angelica said quietly.

"Prince Fenderon was sorry he'd allowed such an uncivilized group of wanderers to stay near the farmers in that area. It's why he no longer allows settlers in the Kingdom. Had we not gone to speak with them that day, I suspect great harm would have come to the good people living near their camp."

"We will find him, I promise you," Angelica said touching his hand.

He found an instant comfort from her fingers as they moved over his, and looking into her deep purple eyes, where there had been a cloud there was now warm reassurance.

"Together, I believe we will," he nodded. "My Prince was wise, sending me to find you."

"You doubted his wisdom," she smiled, a statement not a question.

"I did. I wondered how a young witch could possibly be of help to a Warrior of the First Order, but now I am filled with confidence and admiration."

"I won't let you down," she promised. "There is more than one way to rid a realm of a bad intruder, isn't there, Moon?" she softly murmured stroking her cat. "You know what to do while I'm gone, and I'll be back before you know it."

The tone of her voice was almost like a purr itself, and as he watched her and the silver cat lock eyes, he felt the shadow of a shiver.

You are a mystery, and possess great skill, far more than I could have guessed, and more, I suspect, than I can even imagine.

CHAPTER SIX

D arius had offered to put the few items Angelica needed into his bag, and after saddling River he was waiting for her in the pasture. She arrived carrying a large band of thick braided pink ribbon, and Moon was prancing ahead of her.

"Where is your saddle and bridle?" he frowned.

"I have no need for such cumbersome things," she replied with a toss of her head. "The ribbon is for me to hold on to if I need it, but I rarely do. Mostly I just like the way it looks."

As he watched in astonishment, she looped the ring of decorative ribbon over her mare's head, moved it to rest around the horse's neck, and with an easy spring she flipped herself on to Spirit's back.

"You intend to ride for three days with just that ribbon for control?"

"With you to watch out for me, I'm sure I'll be just fine," she replied, her deep purple eyes sparkling up at him.

Not knowing if she was being sincere or sarcastic he decided not to comment, instead pointing to the trees in front of them.

"I'm sure you know the best way through the forest to the main road, so I'll let you lead for the moment."

"I do know an excellent short cut," she nodded, then shifted her eyes back to her silver cat. "Goodbye, Moon. Stay safe, sweet one."

Without warning Spirit suddenly broke into a fast walk, and taking Darius by surprise River immediately began to follow.

"This is going to be an interesting journey," Darius muttered under his breath, but as he stared at her he was captivated by the beauty of the picture.

Dressed in a white and pink flowing dress, Angelica looked almost fairy-like. The sun was catching red highlights in her long dark hair, and seated on the white mare with only the pink ribbon around her neck, the two looked like they'd stepped out of a mystical painting.

You make a striking pair, and you truly take my breath away, but I'm worried. This is a long ride.

"Are you sure your mare is fit enough for this journey?" he asked moving alongside her.

"Do you think I would be riding her if she wasn't?" Angelica retorted.

"Just checking. She's such a beautiful mare, and I wouldn't want to see her fail from exhaustion."

"I can assure you, if any horse should fail from exhaustion it will be River before it will be Spirit."

She sounded annoyed, and wishing he'd kept his mouth shut Darius raised his eyes and looked ahead.

They had walked through a small clearing and were moving towards a thick cluster of tall trees. It looked dark and ominous with barely enough room to enter, and he was sorely tempted to question her.

"Don't worry," she sighed, "I know exactly where to go."

"Reading my thoughts is sometimes charming," he murmured, "and sometimes it's just annoying."

"Exactly how I feel when you doubt me," she quipped.

"I'll try to remember that, but I still can't see how we're going to fit through those trunks. There's no room between them."

"Still he doubts," she said grimly. "Move behind me."

The thicket was fast approaching, and as they neared he made River follow Spirit as she'd asked. A moment later Angelica turned left, moving directly into the trees. Darius grit his teeth, worried there wouldn't be enough space, but as he turned to go in after her he discovered the trunks were bowed, allowing plenty of room to pass through.

Once on the other side he discovered a carpet of green grass, shards of light piercing the overhead branches, and a wealth of open areas offering more than enough space to move freely around the forest. Spirit slowed, giving him time to catch up, and as they began walking side-by-side Angelica smiled up at him.

"I call this my Castle Green," she beamed. "It's an excellent place to hide if I ever need to, or if I want to spend time without interruption just listening to the trees and watching the various creatures that live here."

"Why would you need to hide? Surely the villagers are blessed to have you."

"Most feel that way," she nodded, "but sometimes…"

"Sometimes?"

"I'd rather not say," she replied, and he saw a tinge of pink cross her face.

"I assume it's because you get up to mischief," he chuckled.

"I don't call it that," she quipped. "There are certain things I see that require, shall we say, uninvited attention."

"Like?"

"Like…there's a nasty little boy who teases animals and bullies the girls. No-one will do anything about it, so I did. They may figure that out and come looking for me. I can stop them of course, but it's better to disappear until things come off the boil. Everyone thinks this forest is impassable."

"They don't know about the bend in the trees?"

"The bend in the trees isn't there unless I ask for it."

"You made those trees bow out?"

"No, I said the bend isn't there unless I ask for it."

"You know what I meant," he said crisply.

"I do," she giggled, "but it's fun to watch your face turn red when you get exasperated."

"Are you going to answer me?"

"I suppose I should. I don't want you to burst a vein," she grinned. "I don't make the trees bend, they bend for me because they want to."

"No, no, this is too much for me to believe," he exclaimed. "It's just too much!"

"As you wish," she said airily. "We'll be at the road shortly."

"The road? We'll be there so soon? That saved us a quarter pass of the suns, maybe more."

"That's why it's called a shortcut," she winked, "and once we reach it there's a turnoff that will take me to my aunt's house. I need to stop in."

"Is it important?" he asked anxiously, not wanting to waste the time they'd just saved.

"I have to stop," she replied. "There are some herbs I need."

"That's convenient. All those bottles and jars and you didn't have what you needed?"

"I thought I did, but then I, uh, discovered I didn't," she replied her eyes staring into his.

"I think there's more to the story. It's fine that you want to see your aunt, but needing herbs? I think that's the excuse."

"Think what you like," she quipped, *and now I know what he means. It is annoying when someone can see through you. I'd better think about something else. Moon, I'll think about Moon and send him a message.*

"Why don't you tell me the real reason you want to see your aunt, and what's her name?"

"Her name is Namia, Aunt Namia."

"That's the answer to the last question, what about the first?"

"I need those herbs," she replied. "I do, I really do."

"I'm sure, but besides the herbs, why do you want to see her?"

"Don't you ever give up?" she exclaimed spinning her head around and scowling up at him. "You're relentless! Why do you have to know absolutely everything? Can't I have some privacy? It's none of your business!"

"My goodness, what a temper you have. Couldn't you have simply said, yes, there is another reason I want to see her but it's personal? You could have tried being polite, or is that not in a witch's nature?"

"Would that have satisfied you?" she snapped.

"Now who's doubting, and must you be so testy?"

"If I hadn't promised not to put a spell on you, you'd be in big trouble right now."

"Oh, is that right?" he chuckled.

"Yes, that's right, and if you keep pestering me, and laughing at me, and doubting me, I will break my promise, and then you'll be sorry!"

"Maybe," he said slowly, "but then you'll have a very sore bottom from a very hard spanking, and you won't get to meet Princess Lizbett and Lord Larian, or stay in the Palace as a guest of Prince Fenderon."

She was suddenly glad of her underthings. The mention of a spanking had sent a strange churning in her stomach, and a surge of moisture between her legs.

"Nothing to say? No angry retort? No threats? Ah, I see the road ahead. Thank you for the shortcut, Angelica. Most impressive."

It was clear she was going to pout so he let her, and as their horses carried them briskly down the road, Darius decided to center his thoughts on Zanderone. Such pondering was safe. If she crept into his head she would find the hallways rather boring.

The attacks had been random. The man was either wandering aimlessly and finding his victims when the opportunity presented itself, or he wanted it to appear that way, and was a stalking, calculating, methodical killer.

Why did the traps we set for him fail? Was he clever enough to know he was being baited, or was he just not in the area? That was such a delectable kiss, and her breasts, her breasts are so full and fleshy. I would love to pull her off her horse right this minute and ravage her.

Blinking rapidly, shocked that his desire for her had burst into this thoughts, he shook he head and wiped his hand over his face.

How did that happen? Did she make that happen, or am I just so drawn to her my lust snaked its way into my head?

Deciding to risk a glance, he stared down at her.

"I can feel you looking at me, and I have no desire to speak to you," she declared, *and in spite of my promise I think I just might send you a teensy weensy dose of my witchery. Not a spell, not really a spell, just a quick incantation. Yes, I will.*

You needed me and we did meet
Now you'll feel the heat in your seat

"Why are you wearing that naughty grin, Angelica?" he asked studying her face. "I may not be a warlock, but I know a mischievous look when I see it."

"I don't know what you mean," she replied suppressing a giggle.

A moment or two passed, and she could see him reaching to the back of his saddle and feeling the leather, but suddenly, her own bottom began to feel unpleasantly warm, and Spirit tossed her head.

What? Oh, no, the spell's coming back to me. Don't worry, Spirit, I'm pulling it off right now.

You needed me and we did meet
Now quickly take the heat from our seats.

The warmth began to recede, but when she risked a glance up at him she was met with a scowl.

"Angelica!"

"What? I told you, I'm not speaking to you," she replied trying to sound like her usual, confident self.

"Is there something you want to tell me?"

"No," she said brusquely.

"I may not be able to invade your thoughts, but I wasn't born yesterday, and I've been around some very conniving women. Don't think you're going to get away with that."

"It wasn't anything," she quipped. "A bit of fun, that's all."

"Angelica," he began, "you need to listen to me very carefully. I think you're a very attractive young woman, and before you start on about how you're not a young woman, take it from me, you are. You may be a witch, but you're still a very lovely, very sexy young woman. You're also obstreperous, willful, and full of mischief. Before you made my saddle hot, I was thinking about how much I enjoyed kissing you, and how I'd love to be naked with you. I don't know if you picked that up, and that's why you decided to-"

"NO," she blurted out, then feeling embarrassed she lowered her voice and added, "if I'd known that I wouldn't have cast my spell."

"Is that your way of apologizing?"

"I guess, I mean, I do apologize, and do you, uh, really want to be naked with me?" she stammered.

"I do, very much."

"Is it true what they say about you, I mean, about the Zanderonian warriors. Are you trained in the art of pleasing a woman?"

"Yes, we are trained. It can be an important part of warfare."

"What? You're trained so you can seduce women to help you win battles?"

"Uh, well, yes," he frowned, "but-"

"That's horrible. I was right the first time. I don't want to speak to you anymore."

"Angelica, we are also trained so we can be sure the women we marry are happy and fulfilled. A harmonious household is imperative for a warrior, but besides that, do you know how many battles have been lost because of women seducing men?"

"I am not talking to you about this. It's horrible, plain and simple."

"You won't think it's horrible when you experience it," he mumbled.

"I never will," she spat.

"You have a very short fuse," he said grimly. "How soon before we reach the turnoff to your aunt's house?"

"It's just up ahead," she said tersely. "Why?"

"Because, my dear, Angelica, you need to be spanked, and once we leave this main road that's exactly what's going to happen."

CHAPTER SEVEN

Angelica could not believe she was once again across his knee. He had yanked down her underwear, and his hot hand was slapping her upturned backside.

"OW. Stop it! OW."

"You can behave as you wish with other people, but with me you will show some respect."

"OWWWW."

"You'll control that short temper of yours, especially once we're in Zanderone. Do you understand?"

"Yes, yes, I do," she wailed.

"No more childish outbursts or pouting," he continued, dispatching his palm to her sit spot, "and in the house of the Princess and Lord Larian, you will be on your very best behavior, or believe me, I will spank you in their presence."

"NOOO!"

"Yes, I won't hesitate," he warned, then pausing for a moment he stared at her very pink cheeks. "I believe I have made my point."

"You have, you have!"

"You will just rest there for a moment, and feel the pain of my punishment."

"Please, will you rub it?" she bleated.

"No, not for a moment or two."

She could have muttered an incantation as he'd pulled her off Spirit and thrown her over his shoulder, or stopped herself from feeling the sting and faked her way through the entire spanking, but she hadn't able to bring herself to do it, and with the hot seat spell bouncing back at her she wasn't sure if it would have worked anyway.

What's the matter with me? I need to speak to Aunt Namia. I hope she can give me some answers.

The unexpected, soothing caress of his hand elicited a deep sigh, and longing for his touch she spread her legs.

"You're asking me to touch you," he mumbled. "I'm not sure you deserve it, and if your pussy is as sharp as your tongue it might well give me a nasty cut."

"I'll be good, I promise," she whimpered.

The temptation of her glistening cunt was too strong, and running his hand over her hot cheeks he continued it down and cupped her feminine charms.

"My, you are not just a mischievous witch, you are a wanton witch. A wanton, wet witch."

"Ooh, those words," she breathed.

His cock was standing at attention, and as he slid his finger into her succulent depths and began sliding it in and out, he ached to kneel behind her and plunge his cock home.

"You are so needy," he murmured. "I will bring you to your moment, but it is not just for your benefit. I need a more temperate companion. The release will calm you down, and that, you naughty witch, is something you need to do very badly."

"Thank you, Darius," she stammered, "thank you."

"Kneel on your hands in knees in front of me, and keep that skirt at your waist."

He was seated on a fallen tree trunk, and as she crawled off his lap he dropped the front flap of his trousers. Pulling his cock from the confines of his undergarment, he gazed at her reddened moons and slipped two fingers inside her hungry sex.

Rubbing himself as he frigged her, enjoying the sight of her swollen pussy lips and the sound of her pleasure-filled moans, he could feel his climax quickly building. When she let out a wail and thrust back, he chased his orgasm, exploding seconds later with a powerful eruption that rattled his bones.

Having nothing with which to clean his hands he rose unsteadily to his feet, and walking the few steps to his horse he pulled his soiled shirt from his saddle bag.

As he cleaned himself up, he glanced across and saw her laying on the soft ground, her skirt still around her waist. Quickly stuffing the shirt in back in the bag, he hurriedly returned and knelt at her side.

"Angelica, are you all right?"

Rolling over she gazed up at him with half-lidded eyes.

"I am very all right," she sighed. "It's strange, this peace I'm feeling."

"Come to me," he said tenderly, and sitting back he pulled her into his broad chest, engulfing her with his powerful arms.

"Why do I feel this way?" she mumbled.

"A good spanking followed by a release can have this affect," he replied. "I told you it would calm you down."

"Why? It's so strange."

"We don't always need to know the why of something. Just accept it and be grateful."

"I am," she sighed. "I feel so relieved, as though all the tightness has left me."

"Rest for a moment, then fix yourself, and we'll continue on to see your aunt."

Closing his eyes he felt her mold into his body. A warm, comforting light was beginning to dawn in his soul, and he let out a heavy breath.

Is this the end of my years of wanting? Does this adorable, naughty, willful witch hold the key?

"I feel awake now," she said stirring in his hold. "My aunt's house is close. I shall ask her for some glow tea and something to eat. I'm hungry."

Releasing her from his arms, he pushed himself from the ground then helped her to her feet.

"What is glow tea?" he asked as he brushed the twigs and dried leaves from her dress and plucked them from her hair.

"It is a tea that refreshes and brings fresh energy," she replied. "It is a combination of many roots and flowers. I have some with me, but I'd prefer to save that for our journey, and my aunt can serve hers to me hot, with honey."

"It sounds like something I could use as well," he grinned as they walked to their horses.

"Yes, I'm sure you could," she giggled.

Mounting up they started on their way, and though there was little conversation, there was a new comfort between them, and they could both feel a burgeoning closeness.

They rode through a wide meadow, across a shallow creek, and up a gentle slope, and as they reached the top Darius could see a smattering of farms and homes below.

"Aunt Namia lives in that first house, the big one with the tall brick fence around it."

As they started down, Darius was surprised at the size and impressive look of the home. He had always thought witches and warlocks lived by their wits, and had difficulty making enough coin with which to survive. Angelica certainly didn't seem to suffer such a life, and apparently, neither did her aunt. Approaching the house he saw the front door swing open, and a tall, green-haired willowy woman come out to meet them.

"Angelica," the woman called. "I'm so happy to see you."

They climbed off their horses, and the woman hurried forward to unbolt the heavy gates. As they swung open Angelica ran to her, Spirit at her side, and hugged her tightly.

"This is Darius, he's a Zanderonian warrior, a Warrior of the First Order to be precise. Darius, this is my Aunt Namia."

"Very pleased to meet you," he said.

"Come inside, have some tea, and tell me why you're here, though I can see it already," she remarked staring into Angelica's eyes. "Yes, you and I need a private word."

"Thank you, Auntie," Angelica sighed.

"Darius, you may let your horse loose here in the front. There is no way out with the gates closed, or you can tether him to the side of that shed if you prefer."

"Uh, I'll have to unsaddle him if I let him loose," he mumbled not sure what he should do. "We won't be able to stay very long."

"Five minutes without a saddle is better than nothing," Angelica said softly.

"Yes, you're right. It will only take me a minute."

"I'll prepare some tea and something to eat," Namia smiled. "Just come in when you're ready."

As he began to unfasten River's girth, he watched Angelica and her aunt walk inside, arm-in-arm.

"I shall be in a house with two witches," he muttered. "Will any of my thoughts be private? What an adventure this is turning out to be, and it's only just beginning."

CHAPTER EIGHT

"So you see, Auntie, I don't know what this means," Angelica said urgently as she sipped her tea. "I can't read him, at least, not very well, and I feel so needy for him. I've never felt needy, not ever."

"I attempted a peek into his head myself," her aunt replied. "I felt the resistance, but I could have pushed through, and yet you can't. There are several reasons why you might be having this trouble."

"Is this bad for me? Should I go home? I don't want to. I want to help find the man who is terrorizing the people of Zanderone," she said earnestly. "I want be with Darius, and the truth is, I want to be with Darius more than I want to go to Zanderone. Does that make me a terrible witch?"

"No, but we should always help when called upon. You would still go, wouldn't you, even if you didn't have these strange feelings towards Darius?"

"Yes, yes I would."

"There are you then."

"So tell me, what does all this mean. Tell me, quickly, before he comes in."

"He may well have the warlock gene and it's just dormant. Many do. In the days when witches and warlocks were hunted, many hid their nature. They married, and never told their offspring, and you know it's difficult for a witch to read the thoughts of another witch or warlock. I think I could have, but I'm stronger than you."

"How can we find out?"

"If you can get a drop of his blood I can find out very easily."

"You can?"

"Yes, and so can you, I'll give you some of the powder. Mix equal part blood, powder and water, and if it turns purple he has the warlock gene."

"You said there were other things."

"I wish we had more time," her aunt frowned. "He may have developed this cloaking ability through his training as a warrior, but it may also be that you and he…perhaps I should not say."

"What, he and I are what?" Angelica insisted. "You must tell me."

"I don't wish to influence you, but if it's meant to be, knowing probably won't interfere. Angelica, you and Darius may be cosmically connected."

"What does that mean, cosmically connected?"

"I'm surprised you don't know. It means a couple has been ordained by the stars to be together. By the very nature of this cosmic blessing you would not be able to read him clearly, and your spells would fall weak, or fail, or turn back on you."

"Ooh, I think that's happening already," she whispered glancing at him through the window, "and now he's coming in. I wish we could talk more."

"Time will give you the answer, but the powder can tell you if he has the gene."

"What a charming home you have," Darius declared as he wandered in to join them.

"Thank you. I have some tea and lemongrass cake for you," Namia said moving from the table to fetch his mug and plate.

"Excellent, thank you," he smiled sitting down.

"Auntie, I need some blinding dust," Angelica said as Namia placed the cake and tea in front of Darius.

"Be careful with it," she warned. "You know how powerful it is."

"I will. I may not have to use it, but I want a full arsenal. I have the numbing crystals, the sleeping drops, and the confusion compound, but it's better I have the blinding dust and not need it, than find myself in a situation where I wish had it with me."

"Yes, you're right," Namia nodded. "I'll be right back."

"You're carrying so much," Darius remarked.

"I also have a powder that attracts a hateful heart, and our prey definitely has a hateful heart. We have to draw him out. He won't just walk up and introduce himself."

"No, he certainly won't," Darius frowned as he bit into the cake. "Angelica, this cake, it has so much flavor. Do all witches cook like this?"

"Our recipes, like our family book of spells, is passed down from generation to generation, so in my family, yes," she laughed.

"I feel truly blessed to have you at my side," he smiled at her, "but you must keep your promise. If there's danger, you must stay back."

"If there is danger, I will," she nodded, *but how you see danger and how I see danger is very different.*

As he drank his glow tea and ate his cake, he continued to scan his surroundings. He would never have guessed the house belonged to a witch, though he wasn't sure what a witch's house was supposed to look like.

Wrapped branches hanging from the ceiling, a cauldron in the fireplace, I don't know. This is just so…normal.

"I know you're in a hurry so I won't insist you stay, but on your journey back I expect you to stop in for a longer visit," Namia declared as she bustled back into the room and handed two pouches to Angelica. "The red one contains the blinding dust."

"Yes," she nodded, "I remember. Red, for stop, be careful."

"Exactly."

"The other?" Darius asked casually.

"Just, uh, something else that might come in handy," Angelica replied. *I will tell you, but later. I can't just announce that you might be carrying the warlock gene.*

They chatted a short while about the fear pervading Zanderone. Angelica explained to her aunt how she had used the metal band to visualize its owner, then excitedly gave her the news that they would be spending their first with Princess Lizbett and Lord Larian Lobergene, then staying at the Palace.

"That is exciting news. My niece, a guest of one of the royal family of Verdana, and then of Prince Fenderon himself."

"I hope we catch this nasty man quickly so I can enjoy some of my time there," Angelica remarked.

"I wish we could stay longer," Darius said finishing his tea and cake, "but I'm afraid we must be on way. Please excuse me. I must go and saddle River."

"It was very good to meet you, Darius. Take care of my niece. She can be a bit headstrong sometimes."

"I hadn't noticed," he chuckled standing up. "Thank you for the refreshment, it was outstanding."

They watched him head outside, then Namia reached for Angelica's hand.

"He is a good man," Namia said softly, "but he has strong energy. I would not tease him too much. I know you like to do that, and it's fine to have some fun, but don't push your luck."

"I'm finding that out," Angelica blushed.

"Yes, I sense that you are," Namia nodded. "Go now, you must not keep him waiting. His mission is important and he feels the pressure."

Namia walked her out, watched her jump on Spirit, then waved goodbye as they rode off through the gate.

As they made their up the hill and down through the creek, Darius could feel the rejuvenating effect of the glow tea, and by the time they had reached the main road he felt completely revived.

"That tea and cake, they carry a powerful punch," he remarked.

"We have many excellent remedies for all kinds of things," she smiled.

"Pity you don't have something to take the burn out of your backside," he grinned. "I could see you sitting uncomfortably at the table."

"I agree," she exclaimed rolling her eyes, *and I'll never tell you this, but I secretly love it. I don't know why, and I think I must be quite mad, but I do.*

Their journey continued uninterrupted, and when they came across a clear straight path they allowed their horses a gallop, but only a short one, wanting to conserve their energy and pace for the long ride.

Darius was amazed at Spirit's speed, and the way Angelica rode her with such ease. They talked about Angelica's life in the village, and Darius finally asked something that had been on his mind since he'd first seen her cottage, and again when he'd been in her aunt's house.

"I was under the impression that witches scraped out a living, that they spent much of their life in hiding, but you and your aunt, you live in very nice homes and don't seem to be wanting for anything. Can you explain this please, it's very perplexing?"

"What you describe is how it was in the past, and some witches still hide their nature and do other kinds of work. Some marry and keep it a secret, they don't even tell their offspring, but they still have keen instincts and special skills. To make a living as a witch, you have to be raised as a witch, and remain dedicated."

"You're saying that your witchcraft is like a business, that you sell your spells and things."

"Yes, but we would never sell our spells or incantations. We cast spells for clients, but only if the person buying our services is pure of heart and has good motives. I heal people, I help their difficult animals, I do sell herbs for cooking, and that's very successful."

"I can imagine," he chuckled. "I had no idea. Are there many of you?"

"Not many like Aunt Namia and me. It takes years of study and learning, just like it took years for you to become a Zanderonian warrior. It's just the same, but I do confess I am young, and I have much more to understand. Aunt Namia is my teacher. I go to her with difficult cases."

"Is that what you needed to talk to her about today? A difficult case?"

"Yes, sort of," she mumbled. "The suns are passing. Are we far from where will be spending the night?"

"Not far at all. The village is large, it's more of a town really, and there are three places that offer lodging there. We're staying at the nicest place, of course. It's a big house owned by a widow. She's always very pleased to see me, and you will have your own room. She has a cook and servants, it's not like an Inn."

"What about Spirit and River?"

"The house has a big paddock at the back, and a stable yard with an excellent manager. They'll be very well looked after."

"It's the one thing I don't like about leaving home," she said soberly. "I worry about Spirit. She doesn't know how to live like other people's horses."

"You won't have to worry in this place, and tomorrow we'll be at Lord Larian's compound, and she will be very happy there, I'm sure."

"I, uh, don't have to have my own room," she said softly, her deep purple eyes gazing up at him.

"Not yet, Angelica," he smiled. "One day soon we will share a bed, but not yet."

"When?" she grumbled. "I don't understand. We both want to lay together."

"I'm not sure when," he said honestly. "I just know it's not yet time."

They had reached the outskirts of the town, and as they moved through the main street, Angelica was surprised by the number shops and the hustle and bustle surrounding her. Horses were tied to rails, and wagons carrying goods and people were rattling along the road.

"I don't like it," she cringed. "It's noisy, and there are too many people."

"Stay close to me," he said protectively. "The house is just a short distance ahead and away from all this."

"My head hurts," she declared. "I need to get away from all the noise."

Glancing down at her he could see her place face was red, and she was wearing a heavy frown.

"Hang on, we're almost there."

Turning a corner he led her down a narrow street, and as the sounds of the town fell behind them, the street opened up and they were facing open fields.

"That's it there," he said pointing to a large red house with white shutters. "Are you all right?"

"I will be," she sighed. "I should have worn my cloak."

They rode under an archway of white wrought iron, and followed the drive up to the front of the house. As they climbed off their horses they were greeted by a kindly man who offered to take Spirit and River into the paddocks.

"No," Angelica said firmly. "Just show me where it is and I'll take her myself. I need to make sure it will suit her, and it must be a place I'm able to look out my window and check on her."

"Very well, Miss," the man said kindly. "She's a lovely mare, I can understand your concern."

"I'll come with you," Darius offered.

"You don't need to," she said looking up at him.

"I know, but I want to," he insisted.

They followed the man around to the back of the house, and Darius saw her visibly relax as she led Spirit into a large field and removed the braided pink ribbon from around the mare's neck. The grass was green and high, and the water barrels clean and full.

Still at the gate, Darius quickly pulled off River's saddle and bridle and set him free to join the snow white mare.

"This will be fine," Angelica smiled as she walked back to join him and the stable manager.

"Tell Veranique to give you room number five," the man said. "You can step out on your balcony and look directly into the paddock."

"Thank you, that's perfect," she sighed. "I feel much better. What's your name?"

"Heath," he said with a slight bow of his head.

"Heath, you have a bad knee. I have something that will take away the pain, and if you apply it exactly as I say, it will be healed in five passes of the moons."

Darius watched the man stare at her in shock.

"How did you know that?" Heath asked, his eyes wide with surprise.

"I saw you hobble when you walked up to meet us."

"It has been bad for many years," he sighed. "I doubt-"

"My mother was a medicine woman," Angelica interrupted. "She taught me many things. I want to do this for you because you saw my heart, you understood my love for Spirit, and you didn't judge me, so now I want to do this for you. I assure you, I can cure what ails your knee."

"I am most grateful," he stammered.

"After I have something to eat and drink I'll come back and show you what you must do."

"I live above the stable. Just knock. That's where I'll be."

"I'll see you soon," she smiled. "Don't worry, your knee will be well."

Carrying his saddlebags in one hand, Darius placed the other around her waist and guided her to the front of the house.

"You didn't want to tell him you are a witch?" he whispered.

"Some people don't understand, they think in the old ways," she mumbled.

"That was so kind," he murmured.

"He was kind to me. I could read him, he's in pain. How could I not help him?"

"You really are a very good witch when you want to be," he smiled. "I'm very proud of you. Maybe I won't have to spank you before bed tonight."

"Whaaat?"

"I'm just teasing you," he grinned.

"Oh, I see," she smiled. *It's getting worse. I didn't hear him think that at all.*

"You look tired. Let's get you fed and watered."

"Yes, I think that's a very good idea," she nodded. *That must be it. I'm just tired, and I was bombarded by everyone's energy when I rode through the town. I'm sure in the morning I'll be back to normal. I'll be able to hear some of his thoughts again. Yes, I'm just tired.*

CHAPTER NINE

Darius didn't need sleep, and while Angelica was in her room getting the rest she needed, he spent the quiet night hours considering the potions she'd brought with her, and how best to use them.

The main city in the Principality of Zanderone was small in comparison to other realms, and it occurred to him if he and Larian could split up and cover two areas at once, it would double their chances of killing or capturing the hateful monster who was terrorizing the citizens, but there was only one Angelica.

As the suns welcomed a new day, it was when they were enjoying their morning meal that Darius shared his thoughts with her. Though she appeared slightly withdrawn she listened attentively, then leaning forward in her chair she nodded.

"I may be able to find a local witch, but if the Prince sent you to find me, he must not have much confidence in the ones who live there."

"I haven't heard of any that live in Zanderone," Darius replied. "There was one at court a while ago, but that didn't last very long."

"It's the handling of the herbs that matter. Larian won't be able to perform any incantations, but I might be able to teach him how to use the various compounds."

"Is it difficult?"

"I can't say it's difficult, but it requires delicacy. I'm not sure a Zanderonian warrior can be described as delicate."

"Hmmm, not really," Darius agreed.

"I'm willing to try though," *and I can't read you at all this morning. I can't even sense how you're feeling.* "I have something for us," she continued, pulling two tiny pellets from the bag that she had tied around her waist. "Being a warrior you probably don't need it," she said dropping the pellets in their mugs, "but my senses tell me it will be hot on our ride today, and this will help our bodies stay cool."

"Amazing. What else do you have in that bag of yours? You weren't wearing it yesterday."

"It was under my clothing. I don't like to it to be visible to the people who live around me. Some of the more aggressive youngsters might decide they want to see what's in a witch's pouch. Now that we're away from there I can have it hanging around my waist. It's much more comfortable."

"I'm sorry you live in fear," Darius frowned.

"I don't, not at all. I'm just careful."

"That's wise," he nodded. "Are you ready? We should start off."

"Yes, definitely ready. When will we reach the home of Princess Lizbett and Lord Larian?"

"Just as the moons are about to ascend. It's an easy ride. No mountains to speak of, just some rolling hills, and there's a small lake we can stop at for our midday meal. There's one thing though," he added. "You can probably guess."

"Why don't you just tell me?" she smiled. *I wish I knew. I have no idea what you're about to say. It's really quite frustrating.*

"The ladies of Zanderone are like the ladies of Verdana. They ride with their legs on one side of the horse, and they certainly would never dream of riding a horse without any saddle at all, as you do. I'm not sure how to handle this."

"I will not put a saddle on Spirit," Angelica said firmly. "She would not be happy, and neither would I. Perhaps I will use another horse when we enter Zanderone. I am able to ride in a saddle and use reins, though it is strange for me."

"You could sit in front of me on River," Darius suggested.

"I would like that," she smiled. "I would like that very much."

"Then it's settled. Shall we get started?"

"Yes, the suns continue to rise," she nodded.

"By the way, how is your bottom this morning? Still tender I hope, or do you have a magic potion for that as well?"

"Uh, yes it is, and yes I do have a magic potion, but it's at home."

"If I ever catch you using it, or doing some other witchy thing to neutralize a spanking, you will have a bigger problem than a sore bottom," he said sternly.

"I won't, I promise," she vowed gazing up at him.

As her clear, deep purple eyes touched his, he could feel her sincerity, but something else as well, though he couldn't quite discern what it was.

"I believe you, Angelica. When you're being a good witch like this, I want to hold you in my arms."

"I wish you would," she sighed.

"I will give you a hug just before we get on our horses," he smiled, "but we must get moving."

"I need to check on Heath before we go, but it will only take a moment or two."

"Yes, you do need to do that," he smiled. "See, you are a good witch. You just need to control that mischievous side of yours."

As Darius and Angelica were getting ready to leave, on the outskirts of Zanderone, in the small fortress on the grounds of the Lobergene compound, Lord Larian was gazing fondly at his naked Princess.

It had been several months since their nuptials, and though Lizbett was subject to a weekly spanking, there were times when she needed additional discipline. Lord Larian was constantly amazed at the young woman's penchant for getting into trouble, and though he didn't wish to bully her, or quash her buoyant spirit, her flagrant disobedience was in need of attention.

The fortress he'd found on the compound when he'd first walked the property was ideal for the times Larian and Lizbett wished to explore their deviant pleasures. It offered a full bed chamber with a four poster bed, and an expansive living area with a long table in front of a large, open fireplace, but up a winding staircase was a third room, a room that he'd dubbed, The Punishment Chamber.

He'd had it furnished with a variety of unique chairs and benches, and would escort Lizbett there whenever she needed to be taken in hand. Heavy cabinets housed a number of items, including straps and shackles, feathers and hand-crafted phallus's of different sizes, along with lotions that were used to sting or to soothe.

Lying on her stomach over a low bench, her knees resting on the floor on either side, her wrists and ankles bound to its supporting legs, Lizbett was gazing at the feet of her warrior. As usual, she had only herself to blame for being in such a predicament.

Larian had been in Zanderone meeting with Prince Fenderon, and not due back until the suns were low in the sky. Lizbett thought it the perfect opportunity to ride Scarlet, her mare, as she wished; legs astride on a regular saddle. The stable hands were forbidden to put such a saddle on Scarlet, so Lizbett had delivered them several large bottles of strong ale at their midday meal. An hour later they were fast asleep.

Delighted her plan had worked, she had taken Scarlet for an afternoon's ride, sure she'd be back before the stable hands woke, and long before Larian returned from the Palace.

Unfortunately for Lizbett, Larian had not dallied to socialize. Knowing Darius and his guest would be arriving at his home for the evening meal, Larian had left the Palace immediately after he had finished his business with the Prince.

As he'd turned off the road and cantered up the drive towards the stable yard, he'd seen his recalcitrant young wife galloping her mare up the hill behind the house.

She was astride a horse as a man would be, and perched on her toes, her body leaning over Scarlet's neck. While he'd thought it a beautiful sight, she had broken her promise. They'd made a pact; Lizbett could ride in such a manner, but only when they were together, and he was sure no-one could see her.

Furious with the stable hands for breaking his command and saddling the horse with a man's saddle, he was shocked to find the empty bottles of ale, and the five young men sleeping soundly in the afternoon sun.

Pushing Thunder into a gallop up the hill, it had been easy to catch up to her, and as she had pulled Scarlet to a stop she'd stared at him red-faced, a guilty look in her light mauve eyes.

"Follow me," he'd said sternly.

She knew where they were going, and a short while later their horses were grazing in the field outside the fortress, and they were inside The Punishment Chamber.

"You're fortunate Darius and his witch will soon be arriving," he said gravely, "or you would be in this chamber until the moons cross in the sky."

"I'm sorry, Sir. It's such a lovely day. I just had to go for a ride."

"To coerce the stable hands into drinking so you could ride as you wish is shameful," he scolded.

"Sometimes I just can't say no to myself," she whimpered.

"What am I to do with you?"

"I don't know, Sir," she mumbled.

"It's been some time since you've had anal punishment," he remarked as he pulled open a drawer of the cabinet.

The sound of her groan told him he'd made the right decision, and selecting a large, solid phallus, he smothered it with a tingling, slippery balm that would ease its entry, but offer a stinging itch. Returning to straddle her back he leaned over, pulled her right cheek aside, and placed the tip against her anus.

"Open up," he commanded.

She had learned it was best to surrender, and moaning loudly she did as he directed. As the beast pushed forward, stretching and filling her, she let out a loud yowl.

"There, let that sit there for a while. Soon the lotion will begin to work and you will regret your disobedience, and I will pleasure myself to the sight of your squirming bottom."

Stripping quickly, he grabbed a chair and settled behind her, relishing the sight of her stuffed behind, and her wet, wanting cunt.

As the tingling began, and she wriggled and moaned, he massaged his member, thoroughly enjoying the lewd sight. The balm would not only drive her crazy, but would make her ache for his cock, and her need began to show itself as her pussy glistened with its dew.

"Such a bad girl," he growled, pausing in his pleasurable massage to land several hard swats. "Not only does your bottom now suffer for your sins, but look at how your kitty cat is salivating, so hungry for attention."

Sliding two fingers into her depths, he moved them in and out, stopping every few strokes to touch the supersensitive button deep in her grotto.

"Oh, Sir, please," she wailed. "I'm so sorry, please let me have my moment."

"Absolutely not. You have been a disobedient, underhanded girl, and you shall be punished as such."

With one hand pleasuring his cock, he used the other to grasp the end of the phallus, and began to pump the wooden intruder, slowly pulling it out, then pushing it back in, stopping every few seconds to swat her backside with hard, hot smacks.

"Sir, I have to come, I have to," she howled.

"The way you had to get those boys drunk today, so you could ride your mare improperly?" he scolded, slapping the backs of her thighs to underscore his reprimand.

His cock was reaching its bursting point, and taking hold of the phallus he slowly withdrew it, then stared down at her dark, open hole.

The tingling lotion would be subsiding, and the intense stimulant would give him a powerful orgasm. Spreading her cheeks he thrust forward, fucking her lustily.

"You are my wife," he thundered. "You will learn to do as you're told."

"Yes, Sir," she cried. "It was wrong, I know it was wrong."

As the moment began to shudder through his loins, he squeezed her cheeks, eliciting a yowl, and when he surged with his final, violent spasm, he could feel her trying to rub the sensitive nub between her pussy lips against the bench.

Falling from her depths he closed his eyes until the delicious prickling passed, then slowly rising he moved across to the wash basin. He leisurely cleaned himself and the phallus as he watched her continuing efforts to rub herself to her release, then carried the damp cloth back to her.

"I will be placing you in ropes tonight, to prevent you from touching yourself," he said as he gently wiped her. "Perhaps, if you are a very good girl while Darius and his witch are here, and I see you are genuinely remorseful, I will bring you to your moment the night they leave."

Untying her wrists and ankles he pulled her into his arms, and as she leaned into him she let out a heavy sigh.

"I really am very sorry, Sir," she whimpered. "Thank you for punishing me. I always feel so much better for it."

"I know you would have told me what you'd done," he sighed. "At some point you would have confessed. At least you have developed a conscience."

"Yes, I have. Sometimes I think there's two of me. One who wants to be good, and one who doesn't, but we both love you."

"I love you both as well," he said tenderly. "We must return to the house and make ready for our guests. You will have a very uncomfortable ride back the house, but you deserve it."

"Yes, Larian, I do, and I'm sorry."

CHAPTER TEN

The woman who had laid the dining table watched nervously as Lizbett slowly circled, scrutinizing every detail. She prided herself in being an excellent hostess, and knowing she would someday be Queen of Verdana, she was cognizant that the dinner parties she and Larian held gave her the opportunity to hone her skills. They had entertained Prince Fenderon and his wife, Princess Alexa, and on several occasions had enjoyed entertaining dignitaries who were passing through the realm.

When Larian walked into the room he found Lizbett ordering the woman to switch the large bouquet of flowers in the center of the table, with a smaller arrangement that had been placed on the sideboard.

"Much too ostentatious for a group of four," she declared, "and it's not comfortable for guests to have to look around the centerpiece. They must be able to look over it at the person seated opposite them."

"Yes, Your Highness, I will do better next time."

Larian broke into a broad smile.

If only the servants could have seen you a little while ago. Your bottom stuffed with a large, irritating phallus, your cheeks red from my spanking hand, and your pussy desperately rubbing itself against the bench.

"You look lovely, Lizbett," he smiled.

"Larian, I didn't see you there."

"I do admire your attention to detail," he remarked walking across to her. "You've become a very elegant, polished young lady, at least some of the time."

"Thank you," she grinned. "I'm very happy you approve."

"It's delightful to see you this way, so graceful and refined. Your mother and father would be very proud. What happened to that spoiled child I married?"

"I'm sure I don't know what you mean," she quipped raising her eyebrows.

"Darius and the witch should be here soon," he said staring out the window. "The suns have descended. I do hope they arrive before the moons begin to pass."

"I made sure Falayla filled the tubs in their rooms. No doubt they'll be very dusty from the long ride."

Falayla was Lizbett's personal servant. The young village girl had been instrumental in helping prevent the assassination of Lizbett's father, King Handerah.

Falayla had risked her life and given Larian the information he'd needed to foil the plot. In gratitude the young maiden had been offered the position of Lizbett's personal servant, and though she'd had no experience, she had excelled in her new position.

"No doubt," Larian agreed. "I'm sure they'll be grateful for a soak."

"I'm very excited about meeting a real witch," Lizbett said enthusiastically. "Falayla is terrified, poor thing. I don't think we'll see much of her while Angelica is here. Have you ever spent time with one. A witch I mean?"

"Yes, more than once, but I understand Angelica is quite young for one so accomplished. I believe she's close to your age."

"It's funny how we think of witches as being old hags," she laughed.

"That's how they used to be, but not anymore. Their talents are finally being recognized and appreciated. They can be a bit unnerving though."

"Why? If they mean us no harm, what's the worry?"

"Many of them can read your thoughts and sense your feelings. The Prince had a witch in residence at the Palace who would tell him when someone was lying. The nobles and courtiers found it impossible and made a fuss. He finally had to excuse her, though he did use her to question a suspect if they were accused of some nefarious act."

"What happened to her?"

"She passed away. Natural causes, just old age, I believe."

"Wow, that's quite a story. I wonder what Angelica will be like."

"I think you're about to find out," he smiled.

The sound of horses entering the stable yard sent them to the front door, and as they stared out at the couple arriving, Lizbett grabbed the sleeve of Larian's jacket.

"Look how she's riding," she whispered. "Astride with no saddle, and, oh, my goodness, no bridle, no reins, nothing. How is she able to do that?"

"Astonishing. That won't go down well in Zanderone."

Walking out into the yard, Larian and Darius hugged each other warmly.

"My friend," Larian smiled, "welcome home."

"It's good be here," Darius grinned. "Larian, Princess Lizbett, may I present, Angelica, and I'm suddenly very embarrassed. Angelica, I don't know your last name."

"Because I don't use one, I'm just Angelica," she replied. "Your Highness, Lord Larian, it is such an honor to meet you both."

"Please, don't stand on formality, call me Lizbett, and please, come inside. Dolfo will take care of your horses."

"I do apologize," Angelica said shyly, "but I must see to my horse myself. I must take her to her paddock. She will not settle unless I do."

"I completely understand," Lizbett nodded eagerly. "Men don't understand how we women are with our horses, and yours is so beautiful. What's her name?"

"Spirit. Would you like to meet her?"

"I would, very much. You men go ahead. Angelica and I have things to discuss."

Slapping Darius on the back, Larian gestured him forward.

"It looks as if it's just the two of us for the moment," Larian remarked as they headed inside. "Do you have bags? There's a tub waiting for you if you wish to soak."

As the men moved into the house, Lizbett stepped forward to meet Angelica's white horse, and as she softly stroked her neck, Spirit turned her head and gazed at her.

"Angelica, she's so wonderful," Lizbett sighed. "I feel as if she's talking to me."

"She is, she likes you," Angelica replied, *and I can't read you. What's wrong with me? I could read your husband, thank goodness, and what a strong man he is, but you, I can't read you at all.* "She'd like to be in the same field with River, if that's possible."

"Of course it is," Lizbett nodded. "Dolfo, put River in the paddock directly next to the house. My guest and I will follow with Spirit here."

The groom had already removed the saddle and wiped off River's back, and began walking the horse across the stable yard. As Angelica followed with Lizbett at her side, Spirit fell into step with them.

"That's amazing," Lizbett remarked in wonder. "How do you ride? I mean, you have no saddle or bridle. How do you have control?"

"Spirit and I have an understanding, and don't forget, I am a witch. Many witches have a unique communication with animals. It's a gift with which I was blessed at birth."

"It's astonishing! She's walking next to you like a person would."

"Of course," Angelica laughed.

"I wish I could ride Scarlet the way you ride her, but I'm not even allowed to sit astride on a saddle. I get in terrible trouble if I do," she said, still feeling the soreness from her punishment just a short time before.

"I couldn't. It's not natural for a witch to ride that way, but I understand most women prefer it," Angelica remarked.

"I know they do, but I never have. I don't know why, but I don't like it at all."

They had reached the paddock, and as Dolfo led River in and removed his bridle, Angelica lifted the braided ribbon from around Spirit's neck.

"This field is for you my sweet girl," she purred. "Eat, rest, drink, do as you wish. Stay near River though, and keep him from harm."

Spirit nickered softly, then dropped her head and rubbed Angelica on her chest before ambling away.

"That was so beautiful," Lizbett breathed. "It almost brought me to tears."

"You're a sensitive soul," Angelica remarked staring into Lizbett's violet eyes.

"Do you think so?"

"Definitely. More than people realize. It's strange, I can't read your thoughts, but I can feel your energy. You're special, Lizbett, I'm just not quite sure why."

"Well, I am a Princess."

"No, it's not that. It's something else. I will ask tonight before I go to sleep. I may have an answer in the morning."

"We should probably join our warriors. Are you all right to leave Spirit?"

"Yes, she's fine. Do you have a tub? I would love to soak the dirt and dust off me."

"We do," Lizbett replied as they started moving back to the house, "and it's filled with rose water, just for you. It's strange, I feel as if we're old friends."

"Yes, I know, I feel the same," Angelica smiled, "and I was so nervous about meeting you."

"And I was nervous about meeting you," Lizbett exclaimed. "I want to hear all about what it's like to be a witch. Will you tell me?"

"Of course I will, and I want to hear what it's like to be a Princess, and to be in love, especially what it's like to be in love," Angelica sighed.

"It seems we have a lot to talk about. I hope you find that horrible man quickly so we can spend some time relaxing together. If Darius is anything like Larian, you'll be on the hunt first thing in the morning and we won't have a chance."

"I suspect we will, and we should be. The fiend must be stopped, but I am truly looking forward to spending time with you, Lizbett."

They had reached the front door, and Falayla was nervously waiting to show Angelica to her room.

"I'm going to take her myself," Lizbett said. "You can go to your quarters. I won't be needing you any further."

"Thank you," Falayla replied, and with a quick curtsy she hurried away.

"She's very nervous about having a witch in the house," Lizbett whispered.

"Not uncommon," Angelica giggled.

Breaking into giggles herself, Lizbett took Angelica's hand and led her through the hallway and up the stairs.

Larian, standing alone and sipping a glass of wine in the living room, had watched the scene play out, and shook his head as his eyes followed them up the staircase.

"That's a first," he muttered. "Lizbett escorting a guest to their room. I can't say I blame her. What a charming and beautiful young woman Angelica seems to be. Hmm, why do I think this is going to be a very interesting few days?"

CHAPTER ELEVEN

When Lizbett ushered Angelica to the guest room, she was shocked when she discovered that the dress laying on the bed was Angelica's only change clothes, and like the dress she was wearing, the long, diaphanous gown wasn't appropriate for the Palace.

"Please let me give you something clean and fresh to wear," Lizbett insisted. "I have so many outfits."

"That is such a kind offer. Thank you. It would be nice not to put this dress back on, and I should save the other for the ride home. I had intended to buy something at one of the markets," Angelica said sheepishly. "I don't like to burden Spirit with anything on her back except me, and when I saw Darius had only those small saddlebags I wasn't sure what to do. I knew I was meeting you, and it did worry me, but then my star guides-"

"Star guides?"

"Yes, that's what I call them, the voices that talk to me, that help me, they told me all would be fine when I arrived, and thanks to you they will be," Angelica beamed.

"That is so fascinating. You stay right there. I just thought of the perfect outfit for you."

As Lizbett hurried away, Angelica wandered across to the window and gazed down at River and Spirit below. The moons were beginning their slow ascent, and Spirit's white coat was glowing under the soft silver light.

"I love you, Spirit," she whispered.

Spirit pricked her ears and lifted her head, then offered a soft whinny in return.

"Here you are," Lizbett said walking back into the room. "This will look gorgeous on you, and you may keep it if you wish. The crimson color doesn't work very well with my red hair, but it will look wonderful on you, especially with your eyes and dark hair. Speaking of your eyes, may I ask what color you call them? I've never seen it before."

"Deep purple, similar to yours, but yours are lighter. I inherited my mother's eyes."

"Can you see through things?"

"Oh, my goodness, no," Angelica laughed, "and just as well."

"Now that I think about it, you're probably right," Lizbett giggled. "I shall leave you to soak and get changed. It's wonderful to have you here. Just come down when you're ready."

Lizbett left her with a warm hug, and the moment the door closed Angelica quickly pulled off her dress and underthings, and slipped into the warm, rose-scented water.

"This is heavenly," she mumbled as she sank down and closed her eyes.

Sighing heavily, images of Darius wandered through her head. The way he made her feel weak and wonderful brought a smile to her lips, but she was disturbed that she was no longer able to read him.

I can't read Princess Lizbett's thoughts either, and that is very peculiar. She's nothing like I imagined. She's so bright and bubbly, and so sincere. I'd heard she used to be impossible. Has being married to Larian made that much difference? I can feel their closeness. The pink and red energy between them is remarkable. At least I can see that. Larian consciously blocks me, but I can feel that he's been trained to do that. Darius, though, that feels different. I must stop this. My head is spinning too much.

"Let me rest, bring me peace
Still my mind, my thoughts release."

As she spoke the short incantation, her mind fell into nothingness, and she felt her muscles relax in the soothing, fragrant water.

Downstairs in the beautifully appointed living room, Darius had joined Larian and Lizbett, and the three were sitting around a low fire. A pitcher of fruit wine and some bite-sized morsels sat in the center of the stone slab table in front of them. The conversation had turned from the journey Darius had just completed, to the reason he was there; the apprehension or elimination of the villain terrorizing Zanderone.

"I think I need to give the operation a name," Darius said thoughtfully.

"What about, Operation Hateful Heart," Lizbett suggested.

"That's perfect," Darius exclaimed. "Did Angelica tell you she saw his hateful heart in a vision?"

"No, we didn't discuss your mission at all," Lizbett replied. "The words, hateful heart, just came to me."

"She does things like that," Larian smiled. "It keeps you on your toes."

"I'm sure," Darius chuckled, "and speaking of Operation Hateful Heart, I was thinking we'd be more effective if we were on opposite sides of the city. He has struck in the farming community, but only once. I think he lurks by the Palace."

"I agree. I believe the city is his hunting ground," Larian nodded.

"We need to use Angelica's concoctions to lure him out," Darius said thoughtfully, "and we may need them when we find him. I know we are mighty in battle, but I fear this man has weapons we have not faced."

"Like the spinning blade?"

"Exactly," Darius grimaced. "it was lethal, and he may have other dreadful things. Angelica has offered to teach you about her potions so you can safely handle them. I was thinking, if she's not too tired, she could show you after dinner."

Lizbett had been quietly listening, and leaning into Larian she gazed up at him and touched his arm.

"Perhaps I could be the one to learn about the potions. You and I could-"

"No, absolutely not," Larian said firmly. "It is much too dangerous, I won't hear of it."

"I am familiar with the handling of herbs," she pressed. "You know I've started my own small garden at the side of the house."

"I'm sure you could handle them well enough, but this scoundrel is a murderer, and goodness knows what else."

"I'll be with you," she argued. "You can protect me."

"No, and that's the end of it," Larian said sternly. "I will not have you at risk."

Angelica was walking down the stairs and overheard the conversation, and as she walked into the living room she felt the force of the fierce protective energy Larian was emitting.

He is completely attached to her. He would fall apart if anything happened to her, anything at all. His guilt would consume him. He would blame himself.

"Angelica," Darius said standing up as she entered the room. "You look..."

Lost for words, he stared in awe at the beautiful young woman gliding towards him. The dress Lizbett had given her was soft red, almost transparent, and flattered her curves. Gold thread was woven through the fabric and glistened from the fire's light, and her deep purple eyes shimmered like rubies touched with a lavender hue. She had applied some fruit stain to her lips and across her cheek bones, and her hair, having been dampened by the water in the tub, had sprung into gentle curls.

"Thank you," she smiled, and feeling his admiration, a warm spontaneous blush rippled through her being.

"You look amazing," Lizbett said happily, standing up and moving towards her. "Please, come and sit down. We were just talking about the mission."

"We're calling it, Operation Hateful Heart," Darius announced still staring at her as she settled into a chair.

"That's an excellent name," she nodded.

"Lizbett's very clever suggestion," Darius said.

"I was just saying that I should join with Larian, and be the one to handle your potions for him."

"I said no," Larian said brusquely.

"If you say so," Lizbett said airily, "but perhaps can talk about it more after dinner."

Angelica almost laughed out loud at the look on Larian's face. Lizbett's quiet determination to change his mind was exasperating, but she was so sweet in her relentless pursuit to get her way, Larian didn't know quite how to handle it. Glancing across at Darius she saw him covertly grinning, but the sound of a gong interrupted the amusing moment.

"Dinner is served," Lizbett declared. "I've arranged for a variety of dishes. I hope you find something to your liking."

"I'm sure I will," Angelica smiled. "I am very hungry after our long ride."

As they stood up and moved into the dining room, Lizbett paused, lifting her nose to the air.

"What is it?" Larian asked.

"Can't you smell that?"

"You and your nose," he chuckled. "Darius knows about this of course," he said to Angelica, "but Lizbett has an extraordinary sense of smell. It was what saved her father's life. She smelled the poison in the soup. It was virtually undetectable by anyone else."

"Fascinating," Angelica remarked.

"I told the cook specifically not to use the root of the ambercum," Lizbett frowned. "It doesn't sit well with me. I hope she hasn't put it in all the dishes."

"Ah, ambercum, it is highly acidic," Angelica agreed. "It does have a wonderful flavor, but it must be used sparingly."

Three servants appeared, each carrying a covered bowl, and after placing them on the table, one of them stepped forward to lift the lids and describe their contents.

"The first, fish poached in wine, baby onions and lemon. The second, fowl in a rosemary and cream sauce, the third, game in a thick meat gravy. Additional vegetables will follow."

"It's the game," Lizbett declared.

"That's impressive," Darius remarked. "I have an outstanding sense of smell, but nothing like yours. I can't detect it at all."

"She's never wrong," Larian grinned.

As the dinner continued, Angelica caught Darius sending her admiring glances, and each time she would gaze back at him with a silent thank you.

Sensing the attraction between them, Lizbett thought they'd make a stunning couple, and promised herself she would do whatever she could to encourage their friendship.

After the dessert had been served and thoroughly enjoyed, Larian suggested they move to the living room for tea.

"Are you too tired to teach me about your potions?" he asked Angelica as they rose from the table. "I certainly understand if you are."

"I am a bit weary," she admitted, "but this is important, and I'll know very quickly if they will be safe with you. They are potent and can harm the handler. I wouldn't want anything to happen to you."

"Ah, I see," he nodded.

"I'll just go to my room and fetch them," she smiled.

"I'll come with you," Darius said quickly. "I'd, uh, I'd like to ask you something."

As Angelica and Darius headed up the stairs, Lizbett walked over to stand next to her husband.

"Larian," she whispered.

"The answer is no," he said firmly.

"Larian," she whispered again.

"What," he said fighting a smile as he looked down at her.
"If you can't handle the herbs properly, what then?"
"You need a spanking," he said softly into her ear.
"I just had one, and that's not an answer," she murmured.
"No, but it will do for now."

CHAPTER TWELVE

Opening her bedroom door, Darius gestured for Angelica to move ahead of him, then closing it behind him he grabbed her elbow and spun her around.

"You take my breath away," he growled, "and I know it's not from any spell."

"Darius," she whispered staring up at him.

Clutching her arms in his strong hands, he gazed into her glimmering eyes, and suddenly his lips were on hers. He pressed urgently, moving his mouth with a hot, ardent passion, his need rising up as he consumed her, his heart pounding in his chest as he tasted her, and every part of his being ached to possess her.

"Darius," she gasped as he broke his grip to engulf her in his powerful arms.

"It is a spell," he said in a sharp whisper, "it is Cupid's spell. I am enthralled by you."

"I am under Cupid's spell too," she whimpered. "I am weak against you, I am only happy when I think of you and when I am in your arms. I wonder, all the time, how it would be to lay with you, and I want you so badly it hurts."

"Your words thrill me," he breathed, "and when our mission is behind us, you and I will have our time together, and it will be the first of many, I promise you."

A deep emotional wave washed over her, and tilting her head back she studied his face.

"Something has happened to me," she murmured. "I can no longer read your thoughts. It's puzzling, and the hot seat spell I cast when we were riding, it bounced back to me. I spoke to my aunt, and she said it must be one of three things. Did you train to protect yourself from a witch's probing mind?"

"No," he said shaking his head. "A warrior can focus and block things out, but that is the extent of the training."

"Please prepare yourself for what I am about to say next," she warned. "You might carry the gene of a warlock."

"Me? No, I think not," he frowned.

"I can find out very quickly," she said breaking his hug. "I have a powder that can test you."

"Really? Let's do it now, downstairs with Larian, but I'm sure I'm not a warlock."

"I'll get my potions," she said, and moving to the bed she reached underneath and pulled out her leather pouch. It was secured at the neck with a drawstring, and opening it slowly she peered inside.

"They are all still tied properly. It is safe to take them down."

In the living room, Lizbett and Larian had settled on the couch, and a large carafe of nutmeg-cinnamon tea sweetened with honey was on the table with four cups and saucers.

"They're taking a while," Larian remarked.

"Well, of course," Lizbett replied rolling her eyes.

"What do you mean, of course?"

"Didn't you see it?"

"See what?"

"How they were looking at each other over dinner? How Darius chased her up the stairs to be alone with her? I thought they were going to fall on the floor and rip each other's clothes off," she giggled.

"Really?"

"Goodness, Larian, for a Warrior of the First Order, you can be completely unaware sometimes."

"Uh, but, she's a witch. Can a regular man be involved with a witch?"

"I would assume so. If they are in love, why not?"

"I suppose. Yes, you're probably right, but wouldn't he worry about her casting spells on him?"

"I don't think she would, would she? I mean, not if she loved him. Shush, I think I hear them," she whispered.

"Sorry to keep you waiting," Angelica smiled as she and Darius entered the room. "I have several potions here, and one I will use to perform a test on Darius."

"On Darius? What kind of test?" Larian asked.

"To see if I have the gene of a warlock," Darius chuckled.

"You, a warlock?" Larian exclaimed.

"I don't think it for a minute," Darius replied still grinning.

"It's very simple," Angelica said, "and I'll let you do it, Larian, to see how well you can use those large fingers of yours."

Lizbett suppressed a giggle, but she couldn't contain the red blush that crossed her face as she thought about the deftness with which his hands tantalized her body.

"We need a saucer, or a small bowl," Angelica mumbled searching the table for something she could use.

"Here, will this work?" Lizbett offered picking up a saucer from underneath one of the tea cups.

"That will be perfect," she said pulling out a small sack from her large pouch. "Larian, in this bag is a fine powder. Sprinkle out a very small amount, and add an equal part of water. Stir it with this stick, then Darius, you need to prick your finger and drop in the same amount of blood. What I mean is, the same amount of blood as the water."

"Sounds easy enough," Larian smiled taking the bag and stick.

Opening the top he tilted up, but to his shock a large glop of powder dropped on to the saucer releasing a plume of dust. As he brought up his hand to cover his nose, Lizbett hastily grabbed the saucer and pulled the bag from his hand

"Good grief, you'll blow it all over the place if you sneeze," she exclaimed.

Turning her back to him, she carefully held the saucer over the small sack and gently guided the powder back inside.

"If that had been the sleeping powder or blinding dust, you'd either be passed out or unable to see right now," Angelica declared.

"I'm terribly sorry," he apologized. "I didn't expect it to fall out like that."

"It takes a light, delicate touch," she said. "You have to sort of, tap it out. It's hard to explain. The way Lizbett gently directed it back into the pouch was perfect."

"It was?" Lizbett beamed.

"Yes, it was."

"Please hand it back to me, Lizbett. I need to try that again," Larian frowned, annoyed that he'd made a mess of things.

Cleaning the saucer with a napkin, Lizbett placed it back on the table in front of him, then handed him back the bag.

"Now then," he frowned, "I just slightly tip it and...oh, for goodness sake!"

A large portion of the powder had again spilled on to the saucer.

"It's just not your thing," Lizbett said kindly.

Red-faced, Larian handed everything back to her, and watched her return the powder into its container for the second time. Frustrated, he reached for the large decanter and poured himself some tea.

"Crazy," he grunted. "Something so simple."

"Larian, many things appear to be simple but they're not," Angelica said warmly. "I'm sure there are feats you perform as a warrior that seem easy to onlookers, but took years of training to master."

"I suppose," he said grimly.

"It's a technique, and one that's better suited to the delicate touch of a woman."

"May I try?" Lizbett asked looking across at Angelica.

"Of course, if you wish," Angelica smiled.

Lizbett wiped the plate clean, closed the bag by tightly pulling on the drawstring, then holding it upright she shook it gently to make sure all the powder had returned to the base. Tilting it sideways, she opened the drawstring just a crack, then carefully tapped; a tiny amount of the powder dropped on to the saucer.

"Excellent," Angelica smiled. "I couldn't have done it better. Now the water."

Picking up a glass of water, she dipped in her little finger and used the underside of her fingernail as a scoop, then allowed it to drop on top of the powder.

"Yes, that's exactly right. Your fingernails are your measuring spoons," Angelica laughed.

"Lizbett," Larian exclaimed, "you did that with such finesse! You're right, Angelica, it is a task suited to the hands of a woman."

"Exactly," she smiled. "All right, Darius, now we need to prick your finger."

"This is so exciting," Lizbett giggled. "Darius, do you think you have the warlock gene?"

"No, not for a minute," he chuckled. "Do you have a needle?"

"Oh, yes of course," Lizbett replied jumping to her feet.

As she disappeared from the room, Larian stared across at Angelica and shook his head.

"I couldn't control the flow of the powder at all," Larian remarked. "It was too light, it felt like nothing in my hands."

"That's because you're used to wielding a heavy sword," Angelica replied.

"Yes, that makes sense I suppose, but I'm still a bit embarrassed by my clumsiness."

"What will happen to the powder and water if I am carrying the gene?" Darius asked.

"When we add a drop of your blood, the mixture will turn purple," Angelica replied.

"Here we are," Lizbett smiled returning to the room.

The needle was threaded through a piece of fabric, and sitting down she pulled it out to hand it across to Darius, but the needle jabbed her, and a tiny drop of blood fell on to the plate.

"Ouch, silly me, I'll have to do it all again, I'm sorry," she frowned, but as she reached to pick up the saucer, she paused; the mixture was fizzing.

In stunned silence they all stared at the bubbling concoction and watched, mesmerized, as it slowly turned purple.

CHAPTER THIRTEEN

L arian was the first to react.

"I don't know what this means," he muttered putting his arm around Lizbett, "but it's not going to change anything between us."

"I, uh, please, no," she exclaimed. "I don't know what to think. I don't know if it's a good thing or a bad thing."

"Tell us, Angelica, what exactly does this mean?" Larian asked.

"It doesn't have to mean anything," she said standing up and moving to sit next to Lizbett. "To be honest, I should have realized."

"Why?" Lizbett asked still trying to come to terms with what had just happened.

"First, there's your sense of smell. Everyone carrying the gene has something unique about them, some elevated sense. I'm going to assume you inherited this from your mother or father?"

"My mother," she nodded. "Does that mean my mother...?"

"It does. You're mother carries the witch gene, and as you can see it hasn't affected her life one bit, except to make it better, and it has for you as well. Think about it. The gene saved your father's life."

"You're right," Larian declared, "and yours, Lizbett, and mine, and you prevented the Kingdom from going through a terrible time."

"Besides my sense of smell, why else would you have known?" Lizbett pressed.

"I can't read you. That's why I thought Darius might have the gene, I can't read him either."

Though she'd already told Darius she could no longer hear this thoughts just a few minutes before, at the time the importance of it hadn't hit him. Hearing it again he broke into a broad smile.

That's great! Thank goodness.

"What else?" Larian asked.

"A couple of things. One is Lizbett's need to be astride a horse, rather than ride with her legs on one side. It is far more natural, and witches, or those carrying the gene, need to feel they're following the natural order of things."

"Oh, my gosh, my whole life I've struggled with that," Lizbeth declared. "I just hate sitting sideways on Scarlet. It feels so wrong."

"At least we understand that now," Larian sighed, "but as the Princess of Verdana, it's still not appropriate to ride like a man. You do know that, don't you?"

"Yes, I do, but at least now I know why I've always been so much more comfortable that way."

"The last thing," Angelica said hesitantly, "and please forgive me if I'm overstepping, but I have heard that you were, um, not easy as a child, is that true?"

"Not easy?" Larian chuckled. "You should be a diplomat. She was an absolute terror, weren't you, Lizbett? No-one could handle her, and that child grew into a terror of a young woman."

"As children, witches and warlocks have a completely different way of looking at the world. They have far more energy than most, and if that energy is channeled by an older, experienced witch or warlock, the child can be controlled, but if they don't have that specialized guidance they simply run amok.

I don't believe your mother knows she's carrying the gene, Lizbett, or she would have made sure you got what you needed and were raised differently."

"See, none of it was my fault," Lizbett exclaimed staring at Larian.

"Don't think you can use this as an excuse for bad behavior," he warned.

"I wouldn't dream of it," she promised feeling a flurry of butterflies.

"I always knew you were special," Larian said warmly, "I just didn't know how special you really are."

"Does this mean I can cast spells and things?" Lizbett asked eagerly.

"You have no schooling, so no, you can't," Angelica replied. "A witch is born with talent, but without schooling the talent isn't developed. If you want to explore this side of your nature you can, but you must do it with the right people. Like a sword in the hands of an untrained warrior, it can do unintentional harm."

"Like handling your potions," Larian remarked.

"Yes, like handling my potions."

"Um, excuse me for interrupting," Darius piped up, "but can we test my blood now? I really am very curious."

"Of course," Angelica grinned. "Larian, could you please pass me a clean saucer, and Lizbett, wipe off the end of that needle and give it to Darius."

"I still can't believe this," Larian said shaking his head as he lifted one of the tea cups and handed Angelica the small plate.

"It's a lot to take in," Angelica agreed, "but as you said, it won't change anything, not unless you want it to. Now I must concentrate."

Picking up the small bag, with an expertise born from years of practice, she held it an inch from the saucer. Tapping the bottom a perfect puff of powder fell into the center of the plate, then mimicking what Lizbett had done she scooped up a drop of water with the underside of a fingernail and let it fall on top.

"Darius, prick your finger and hold it over the mixture."

They watched, captivated, and when the blood hit there was no fizz, and no change of color.

"I don't know why, but I'm disappointed," he mumbled.

"I'm not," Angelica smiled. *I'm overjoyed. This means we are cosmically connected. I never thought I would be with a man, not properly, not loved and living side-by-side with him.*

"So, if I don't have the gene, why can't you read me, and why did your spell bounce back?" he asked.

"I'll tell you later," she promised, "and I hate to state the obvious, but shouldn't we be talking about what we're going to do tomorrow? Remember why we're here. To catch a killer."

"You're right," Larian said.

"Now that you know I can handle the potions," Lizbett said staring at Larian longingly, "and Angelica can show me what I need to know about them, can I please, please, please come with you?"

"I don't know," Larian frowned standing up from the couch. "Just because you have that gene doesn't mean you won't be in danger."

"I can teach Lizbett a self-protection spell," Angelica offered. "It will only take me five minutes."

"What will it do? How will it protect her?" Larian asked.

"A couple of ways. I have a lotion that I put on my skin that stops biting insects. The spell is similar. This hateful man won't know why, but he'll want to find another victim. If he tries to push through that invisible wall, he'll fall dizzy. As long as you're nearby, it will give you plenty of time to step in."

"I'm still not sure," he sighed. "What do you think, Darius?"

"Two teams are better than one, and if Lizbett can learn how to use those potions, and that spell will keep her safe, then…"

"Your father will have my head," Larian muttered. "I can't believe I'm even considering this."

"Why don't you think about it? I can show her what she needs to know, so if you decide she can come she'll be ready. All we need is a table, and to be alone with no interruptions."

"The dining table will be cleared by now," Lizbett said, "and the servants won't enter if the door is closed."

"Yes, all right, go on," Larian frowned. "I'll talk this over with Darius."

Angelica picked up her large leather pouch, and she and Lizbett headed out, but Larian suddenly marched forward and took Lizbett by the hand.

"Give us a minute," he said quickly, and led her down the hallway and into his study, closing the door behind him.

"What is it?" she asked. "You look upset."

"I know I should let you do this, I know I should," he began. "I can't handle those potions, not for a minute, and I know they'd be very helpful catching this monster, but I am just so worried that something will happen to you. It's not that I doubt you, it's not that I don't think you're smart, and cunning, and will probably save my life again one of these days, but my whole being is focused on keeping you safe and happy. Having you come out on such a perilous mission just goes against who I am."

"Larian," she whispered feeling a lump in her throat, "you love me so much."

"Of course I do," he sighed pulling her into him. "I couldn't stand it if something happened to you. I'd never forgive myself."

"You can't keep me wrapped up in fur," she whispered.

"No, but I can stop you from hunting a savage killer," he said pulling back and locking her eyes. "I know you want to come out with us, but I can't bring myself to put you at risk, I just can't."

"I understand," she murmured. "I'd still like to learn about those magic potions though. Can I at least do that?"

"Of course, and if you want to learn more about witchcraft...good grief...I can't believe I just said that," he mumbled, "anyway, if you'd like Angelica to stay and teach you some useful spells, or whatever, after this business is over that's fine with me, but as far as hunting for the killer, I'm sorry, my love, it has to be a no."

"I just realized something. If I did go with you, you'd spend every minute worrying about me, and that would put you in danger because you'd be so distracted."

"That is absolutely true," he nodded. "I wouldn't be able to focus on anything else."

"Then it's settled. I'll stay here, though I will miss you very much. I can't imagine not having you in my bed. It will be our first night away from each other."

"I just had a thought," he said his eyes lighting up. "We'll be staying at the Palace. There's no reason you can't come with us into Zanderone. You and Angelica can come together the carriage. It's the hunt for the killer under the moons that presents the danger, but you can stay safely in the Palace when we leave after dinner."

"Really? That would be wonderful, and I'd love to see Prince Fenderon and Princess Alexa," she beamed.

"And I'd love to know you'll be in the Palace waiting for me when I return," he smiled.

"I feel so much better," she sighed. "I would have been so lonely without you here, and I know the circumstances are gruesome, but I'll enjoy spending a night or two at the Palace."

"I cannot tell you how relieved I am," Larian said hugging her. "You go with Angelica and learn about the potions, and I'll tell Darius what we've decided."

CHAPTER FOURTEEN

It was some time later that Angelica and Lizbett left the dining room and made their way up the stairs to bed. Darius and Larian had gone walking in the grounds but had not returned.

"It's the way it works with a Zanderonian warrior," Lizbett sighed. "All they need is their Zinyana sleep every few passes of the moons. Larian wanders or works while I sleep."

"At least you know he's here," Angelica said.

"Yes, and sometimes, even though he's not sleeping, he lays next to me. I love it when he does that. Um, Angelica, do you mind if I ask you something?"

"No, of course not."

"You and Darius? Are you, uh…?"

"Oh, yes, me and Darius. My fingers and toes are crossed," Angelica giggled. "Since I can't cast a spell, it's the only thing left for me to do."

"I think he's captivated by you. It's in his eyes."

"I hope so, I really do."

"You sleep well, and I'll see you at the morning meal, then I must give you another change of clothes, and some outfits that will be right for the Palace."

"You're being so kind to me," Angelica said. "Thank you."

"My gosh, you just discovered that I carry the witch gene. It's the least I can do."

They hugged good night, and a few minutes later, after gazing out the window to check on Spirit, Angelica slipped into bed. Closing her eyes she thought about her warrior and how marvelous it would be to feel his hands explore her body, spread her legs, and touch her most exquisite place.

Lizbett, too, was lying in her bed thinking about her warrior, how desperate she was to feel him inside her, and wishing she could drop her fingers between her legs and rub herself to bliss.

He didn't put her in bondage to stop her from doing so, he did it as a kindness. The temptation was so great, and being prevented by ropes was much easier than having to use self-control. Under the covers, her thighs tensing and her pussy aching for relief, she prayed for his quick return.

Outside, ambling through the grounds, the warriors had discussed the mission, finally deciding it would be best to stay together. As powerful as Larian was, there was too much they didn't know about the devil they would be hunting.

"I wish we could be on opposite sides of the city, with you having Angelica's magic potions, but I admit I'm relieved Lizbett won't be out there," Darius remarked.

"Far too dangerous," Larian nodded.

"She will stay put, won't she?"

"What do you mean?" Larian frowned.

"I mean, she wouldn't suddenly take it into her head to sneak out of the Palace and try to find you, would she?"

"I really wish you hadn't asked me that," Larian groaned.

"Why?"

"Because it's exactly the sort of thing she would have done at one time."

"Not now?"

"No, not now, but I'll make sure of it, believe me," Larian said firmly, "and speaking of my lovely Princess, I'd better head up. After tonight's revelation I think I should be with her. I'm sure they'll be finished with their potions and spells."

"You are fortunate to have found such a lovely bride," Darius remarked as they headed back into the house.

"She hasn't been easy," Larian chuckled, "but as you know, I have been in love with her since I was a boy. I see a glint in your eye when you look at Angelica. Is there something growing between the two of you?"

"I believe there is," Darius nodded, "and I was greatly relieved to hear she could no longer read me. Being with a woman who knows your every thought…I'm not sure how that would work."

"I don't think it could," Larian remarked. "Our thoughts are private, and while I want honesty and openness with Lizbett, there are times it's better she doesn't know what's in my head."

"Exactly," Darius nodded.

They'd made their way up the stairs and were about to split off when Larian touched his arm.

"Darius, on this mission, should anything happen to me…" Larian said softly, leaving the fear of his demise unspoken.

"Yes, I will take care of Lizbett. I won't leave her until her family arrives," he nodded solemnly.

"It's a dark thought," Larian sighed, "but a realistic one. This man we're seeking, I feel he presents a greater threat than we know."

"I feel it too," Darius nodded. "We must stay on guard. I'm very pleased we'll have Angelica with us. She will be able to sense his presence, and I believe her magic will be invaluable."

"I agree," Larian said gravely. "Goodnight, Darius. I'll see you when the suns ascend."

Moving into their bedroom Larian stripped quietly as he gazed down at his wife. Her eyes were closed and she was wriggling under the covers, but her arms were over her head, and he knew it was a way to stop herself from touching between her legs.

Perhaps I should allow her release. She needs her rest tonight, and I don't know what will happen on this hunt.

Slipping under the covers he ran his hand down her arm, and smiling softly she rolled over, opened her eyes and gazed up at him.

"Larian," she whispered, "you're back. I'm so glad. I need you with me."

"I know," he murmured moving his lips to hers.

Kissing her softly he stroked her back, then traveled his hand to caress her seat cheeks.

"You were so naughty making the stable boys drink that strong ale," he breathed in her ear. "You won't do that again, will you?"

"No, Sir. I felt such a desperate need to ride Scarlet as I did, and my nature pushed me forward. Now I know why. Angelica has given me something to help me have better control over my urges."

"She has? That's good to hear," he sighed kissing her neck. "Would you like me to slide inside you?"

"Oh, yes, yes, please," she begged, "but I thought-"

"I rarely change my mind about a punishment, but I have."

"I'm so glad," she sighed. "I'm worried about what you're facing, and I need to be close to you. It will be such a comfort."

"To me as well," he mumbled as he dropped his lips to her neck.

Closing her eyes she surrendered to the delicious feel of his hands as they wandered across her body. His mouth journeyed slowly to her breasts, tonguing and nibbling, and when his fingers pressed into her sex she let out a cry of joy.

"You are dripping," he groaned.

"Don't tease me," she bleated, "please, just take me."

As he moved on top of her, she split her legs and lifted her arms around his neck.

"My mighty warrior," she mewled.

"My beautiful Princess," he sighed.

He raised himself to his knees, touched his cock to her hot, hungry entrance, and with a determined, powerful thrust he glided home.

Larian pumped slowly, his hands gripping her hips, and as he listened to her moans and utterances of pleasure, he felt his cock building towards its moment. He paused, shifting his position, tilting her body to change its angle, and as his thrusting resumed, her moans began to change.

His cock was sparking her sex, and each stroke tingled her clit and massaged the hidden pressure point in her passionate valley. Her fingers clutched at his skin, her back arched, and as he lowered his head to devour her breast she let out a guttural wail.

"My moment," she gasped, "it's here."

As his lips wrapped around her fleshy mound, her pussy pulsed against his cock, and holding her nipple in his mouth he felt himself jerk out his cream.

He was shuddering, the ripples convulsing through his body, and still he sucked, refusing to relinquish the sweet, delectable rosebud. He could feel her spasming beneath him and heard her high-pitched cries, and only when she fell limp and his cock slipped away did he lift his head. Stretching out beside her he pulled her against him, and as she curled into his body he stroked her hair.

"My precious wife," he purred.

"My precious husband," she murmured.

"Sleep well in my arms. I will not leave you." *I shall be here when you wake, and I shall return unharmed from this mission. I will not let this devil take me from you, I swear it.*

Inside the city of Zanderone, Lokai skulked against the walls of the Palace. It had been far too many passes of the moons since he'd last struck. No-one walked alone, there were no stumbling drunks on the street, or women making their way home from a visit to a relative, and there were armed citizens traveling in groups in search of him. Killing random citizens had worked. Everyone was scared, and he fed off their fear.

Now he was focused on finding a way into the Palace.

When his tribe had settled on the outskirts of Zanderone, they had planned to take over the realm. They knew the Kingdom had powerful warriors, but they were few in number, and the Zanderonian people were soft and easy to intimidate.

The scheme had been simple. Slowly take over the outer-lying villages, then move into the city, kill off a few of the warriors, bribe some others, and take over the Palace.

They didn't think some missing livestock would cause such a ruckus, and they were shocked when a group of Zanderonian warriors had ridden into their camp, but it occurred to the elders that it was a perfect opportunity to kill them off.

They underestimated the power, strength and speed of the mighty warriors, and in spite of their unique weaponry the settlers had lost the battle.

Lokai had been a boy and had witnessed the skirmish. He had grown up with a deep hatred of Zanderone, and when he became a man he presented his own plan to the elders, another way to take over Zanderone.

They had given him their blessing, and his plan was working. He had succeeded in sending the city into fear. Now it was time to move into the Palace. He would find a way. Lokai was cunning, he moved in silence, and he always found a way.

CHAPTER FIFTEEN

A s the suns rose, Angelica was jolted awake by compelling
need to provide Lizbett with her own set of potions. She
knew the reasons would ultimately reveal themselves and she
would obey the message, but she was worried. After their
morning meal she waited until Darius and Larian had left, then
sought out dense cloth bags from the kitchen. With Lizbett
watching, she made up a complete second set.

"There," she declared placing the last of the small pouches
into a larger one. "They're all clearly marked so you can't get
them confused."

"Do you think I'm going to need them?"

"I don't know," Angelica replied honestly. "I received a
message to make sure you had them, and now you do. Just don't
let Larian see them. If he picks them up he'll probably spill the
lot."

"You're right," Lizbett said with a half-smile, "and I
certainly don't want to worry him. He has enough on his mind."

"I've taught you the protection spell and how to remove it.
Remember, it will make you repugnant, so wait until you're
alone in your room to speak the incantation, and when you hear
Larian return try to remove it before he enters."

"Yes, I'll remember," Lizbett said confidently.

"Now you must take me to Scarlet. With River leaving I need to make sure Spirit has a new friend. I'm sure she'll find Scarlet entertaining company."

"I want the kind of relationship with Scarlet that you have with Spirit," Lizbett said earnestly. "Is it possible?"

"Absolutely. You're more than halfway there already," she assured her.

"I'd better go up and put this pouch in my personal carry purse," Lizbett said rising from the table. "Are you ready to leave? Do you need anything else?"

"I've already brought down the little that I have," Angelica smiled, "and thank you again for this lovely outfit. You're so generous."

"You look fantastic. With your figure you should have a glorious wardrobe," Lizbett declared.

"Where would I wear it?" Angelica laughed.

"We're friends now, and you're going to be receiving many invitations," Lizbett promised. "I'll be down shortly. If Larian comes looking for me, would you please tell him I've just gone up to get my cape?"

"Of course. I'll meet you at the carriage.

Lizbett made her way up the stairs, and entering her bedroom she found Falayla wiping a tear from her eye.

"I don't feel right about not coming with you," she muttered as she picked up Lizbett's traveling cape and placed it around her shoulders. "The staff have been saying that Lord Larian and the warrior Darius are going to try to hunt down that killer in the city, and that's why the witch is here, to help them. Is that true?"

"Now, Falayla, you know Lord Larian and I don't like gossip."

"I won't rest until you and Lord Larian return," she said gravely, handing Lizbett her carry purse. "Please be careful."

"Try not to worry. We'll be back before you know it, and I have a job to keep you busy while I'm gone. Please separate out the clothes I no longer wish to keep. The brand new ones."

"Yes, Princess, and again, please be careful."

"I will, thank you," she said putting the cloth pouch into her carry purse. "Now then, do I have everything? Yes, I believe I do. Goodbye, Falayla."

"Goodbye, Princess."

As Lizbett walked down the stairs she sensed the young girl's eyes following her, and she could feel her worry. Lizbett had become fond of her, and it suddenly occurred to her that Falayla had not been back to Verdana to visit her family since she had moved into the house after the wedding.

I'll make sure she takes a holiday when this is over. I should have thought of it before. She needs to see her loved ones.

As she walked outside she found the carriage waiting, and Larian standing next to Thunder ready to mount up.

"Are you ready, Your Highness," he grinned.

"I am, Lord Larian," she smiled back at him. "We have to give Falayla some time off to visit her family when we return."

"Where did that come from?"

"I just thought of it," she frowned. "I don't know why."

"I think it's very thoughtful of you, and yes, I agree. Now into the carriage with you," he chuckled.

Climbing inside she settled opposite Angelica as Larian closed the door behind her, then looking out the window she watched him mount the big black horse she had come to adore.

"You are very happy with Larian," Angelica remarked. "He is strong with you though."

"I am," Lizbett sighed. "I am very, very happy, and yes, he is strong with me, but I love it. I truly love it."

"I think Darius would be that way with me," she frowned, "and I am surprised to say, I think I would love it too."

"It's the way of the Zanderonian warrior," Lizbett said soberly. "They believe for a woman to be happy, the man must be protective, loving, and yes, strong."

"I don't think that way," Angelica frowned, "but I feel myself changing."

"The love of a warrior like Darius and Larian will do that," she nodded. "For me, it's been wonderful."

"Such an odd thing," Angelica mumbled. "I don't understand it, yet I want it, I almost crave it."

"Yes, it becomes a craving. I couldn't live without it," Lizbett sighed.

The carriage began to move, and Angelica gazed out the window.

"I've never been in a carriage like this," she remarked. "I've never been to a Palace. I hope I please the Prince."

"You look beautiful, and you're so clever, of course you will," Lizbett assured her, then with a smile she added, "I didn't know a witch could be nervous."

"I don't feel this way very often," Angelica admitted, "and I'm very glad you'll be at my side."

Angelica had nothing to worry about. Prince Fenderon and Princess Alexa were just as nervous about meeting her.

Because the previous witch the Prince had allowed in court had caused such an uproar, they had kept Angelica's visit completely confidential. As far as anyone knew, she was a friend visiting Lord Larian and Princess Lizbett.

When the carriage rolled into the courtyard, the Prince and Princess were standing on a balcony high above so they could watch her arrival unseen. As Angelica stepped out, both Prince Fenderon and Princess Alexa caught their breath. She looked nothing like the wizened old witch they'd once known.

Dressed in finery, her beauty was apparent even from a distance, and when they saw Princess Lizbett whisper in Angelica's ear, it was obvious a warm friendship had developed between them.

"I don't think we have anything to fear," the Prince said softly.

"No, Fenderon, I believe you're right," Princess Alexa said with relief.

Uniformed servants led the small group up the steps and through a tall archway, and as Angelica looked around her luxurious surroundings, her eyes grew wide in wonder.

"This is unbelievable," she breathed.

"It is a very impressive Palace," Lizbett agreed. "One day you must come to Verdana with me. The castle isn't quite as grand as this. It's older, but it has it's own special charm."

The Palace's main building had three stories, and a handsome young courtier showed them to their sumptuous quarters on the top floor. The apartments were next to each other, but separated by small foyers, with lockable doors between them.

"Prince Fenderon will be sending for you shortly," the courtier said with a bow. "If you require anything, just pull the hanging cords by any of the fireplaces."

After the courtier showed Angelica and Darius their chambers, they returned to join Larian and Lizbett in the grand salon of their apartment. As a visiting royal, Princess Lizbett was given the finest accommodations the Palace had to offer.

"These the most astonishing rooms I've ever seen," Angelica exclaimed as she wandered around.

"That's what happens when you travel with a Princess," Larian chuckled.

"It's the only reason he married me," Lizbett quipped.

"That and the fact that you are so wonderfully difficult," he retorted.

"If you'll excuse me, I think I'll go back and explore my room until I'm called for," Angelica said, "and I need a few moments to catch my breath before I meet Prince Fenderon."

"I'll escort you," Darius said quickly.

As Lizbett watched Darius usher Angelica through the door that would lead to her apartment, she looked up at Larian with a twinkle in her eye.

"I think Darius is going to catch more than a villain on this trip."

"I think you might be right," Larian agreed, "and I hope so. It's time he found a woman to love"

"I have a feeling they're going to work things out," Lizbett remarked.

"Assuming we get through this mission unscathed," he grimaced.

"You will," she said feeling an unexpected lump in her throat, "because I know you would never leave me."

"No, I won't," he breathed pulling her into his arms, "not ever."

CHAPTER SIXTEEN

Angelica left Lizbett's chamber, and moving through the small foyer she felt Darius gently guide her forward with his hand at her waist. His touch sent a shiver of longing through her body, and unable to contain herself she turned and leaned against his robust chest.

"What is it?" he asked wrapping her in his arms.

"Everything here is so overwhelming, and I'm about to meet the Prince. I'm just a simple witch. I live in a forest. I ride Spirit. I help the villagers. How did this happen? Why did this happen?"

"It happened because your skills have become legendary. You aren't just a simple witch. Lord Larian and I aren't just simple warriors. We are Warriors of the First Order, we have fought many battles and we have years of specialized training. This is why you are here, because you are a Witch of the First Order."

"You make me sound so accomplished, and I don't think I am. What if I fail? What if I can't do what is needed and you and Larian get hurt because my magic isn't strong enough?"

"Angelica," he said softly, breaking his hug and leading her to sit down on small couch. "Where is this doubt coming from?"

"I feel such a big responsibility," she sighed. "When the suns descend we will be out there trying to find this evil man. The mission is real. The danger is real. Somewhere in those streets lurks a monster."

"Ah, yes, this is your first real battle," Darius nodded. "I understand. Your doubt is natural. I have felt it, Larian has felt it, anyone who has ever faced a major challenge has dealt with these doubts and fears."

"How do I get past them?"

"Believe that your instincts, and all the things you have learned, will be there when you need them. You would not be here if you were not up to the task."

Like a glowing fire on a cold winter's night, his words wrapped around her with a warm, gentle comfort.

"I feel what you just said, yes, I believe you're right."

"There will be nerves when we leave the castle, and that's natural. Nerves are good. They keep you alert, they heighten your senses."

"Darius, you have calmed me," she said softly, "and forgive me, but I must do this."

Before he could speak her mouth was on his, and curling up like a kitten in his lap, her arms around his neck, she sank her lips into his with an ardent, moist, loving kiss.

His manhood surged to attention, and his hand traveled to her breasts, kneading and molding. He heard a muffled moan and tried to push his fingers under the bodice of her dress, but a loud knocking on her door broke their moment.

"Oh, no," she groaned. "Did that have to happen?"

"I believe," he sighed disentangling himself from her limbs, "it is well-timed."

"How can you can say that?" she bleated.

"I would rather the knock come before we were sprawled on the floor with our clothes strewn about the room," he chuckled as he strode across to answer it.

"Good point," she mumbled taking a deep breath.

"It's probably the courtier," he said opening the door, and seeing the young friendly face he nodded. "Yes, I thought it might be you. Is the Prince ready for us?"

"He is, and please call me Serendo, I should have mentioned that earlier."

"Thank you, Serendo. Angelica? Are you ready?"

"Yes, one moment," she called back, and hurriedly finding her comb she ran it through her hair.

"I'll just go and alert Princess Lizbett and Lord Larian," Serendo said, and headed to their apartment just a short distance down the wide hallway.

"Okay, I'm ready," Angelica said breathlessly as she joined Darius at the door.

"Do you feel better now?" he asked losing himself in her sparkling eyes.

"Much, thank you."

"There is another way to calm a worried woman," he whispered.

"There is?"

"Don't you know what that is?"

"I'm not sure, no," she frowned.

"A quick, sharp spanking," he whispered.

She couldn't stop the hot flush crossing her face, and as she saw Lizbett and Larian walking towards them, she swallowed hard, hoping the pink on her cheeks would quickly vanish.

"If you would please follow me," Serendo said formally.

"Angelica, you look a bit hot," Lizbett frowned. "Are you feeling all right?"

"Yes, yes, fine, just excited," she replied. "Are we going to be talking about the mission, or is this just to meet the Prince and say hello?"

"The mission. The Prince will want to hear our plans and contribute his thoughts," Larian replied, and glancing down at her he suppressed a smile. He could guess why her face was crimson.

"Our plan is simple," Darius declared. "If a scheme is too complicated there are more things that can go wrong. We haven't had a chance to go through it with you, but feel free to speak up if you see a flaw, or want to add something."

"I understand," Angelica said.

"I will too," Lizbett piped up.

"I have no doubt about that," Larian remarked.

At the end of the hallway they were led down a winding staircase, and after a short walk they stopped at tall, wide, heavy wooden doors. Serendo knocked three times, and the doors were opened by one of the Prince's advisors, an older man in flowing black robes accented with gold trim.

"Greetings," Lizbett smiled.

"Your Highness," he replied bowing. "Please enter. The Prince awaits."

Angelica reached for Darius, and curling her fingers around his hand she found the support she needed. Prince Fenderon was seated behind a highly polished table with papers laid out before him, and he rose to his feet and walked across the room to meet his guests.

"Princess Lizbett, how lovely you look. Lord Larian, Darius," he smiled, "and you must be the famous Angelica."

"Your Highness," she said with a low curtsy. "I'm honored to meet you."

"Please, come to my table. Refreshments will be here shortly."

"Thank you, Sire," Larian replied. "I see you have a map of the city."

"Yes, and I'm anxious to hear your plan and see what magic Angelica has for us."

Moving back to the table the Prince sat at the head, with Darius and Angelica next to each other on one side, and Lizbett and Larian across from them on the other.

"The red marks are where the killer has struck. Except for the farmer, the murders happened in random areas of the city."

"Yes, but fortunately Angelica has solved the problem of where to look for him. We can lure him to us. She has a potion that the killer will be drawn to."

"You do, Angelica?" the Prince asked. "How does that work?"

"It's difficult to explain, but I have an incantation and potion that will prick his senses and pull him in. The metal band you found will strengthen the spell. How does it work? How is a moth drawn to the flame that will cause him to perish?"

"Ah, yes, a moth to a flame. I can understand that," the Prince nodded.

"We will use this magic in a street with no exit," Larian explained. "The killer will be trapped. I will be waiting in the shadows, and when he walks into the street I will step out. When he turns to run Darius will be in his path, then, if he doesn't surrender, we will overpower him. There are several streets that are ideal," he continued, leaning over the map, "but the one nearest the Palace would be the best."

"May I offer a suggestion?" Angelica asked hesitantly.

"Of course," the Prince replied. "That's why you're here."

"The spell will draw him into the street, but I should be visible. He will believe it was me his instinct reacted to. I will move towards him, and when I am close to him I will use my magic potions. This could be anything from throwing blinding dust into his eyes, or blowing a puff of the confusing compound to disorient him. I might even cast a spell to make him hot or dizzy. I think he needs to be weakened before Darius and Lord Larian attempt to tackle him."

"I don't like the idea of you being that near to him," Darius frowned.

"I agree," Larian nodded. "You are-"

"I am a witch," she said firmly, "and I am here because of the things I can do. Believe me, this killer has far more to fear from me, than I do from him."

She had spoken with such profound confidence and determination, the three men stared at each other, not sure how to respond.

"Very well," Prince Fenderon finally said, "I find myself believing you, and I am most grateful for your offer. That's the plan. Darian, Larius, is there any additional weaponry or manpower you need?"

"No, Sire," Larian replied. "More men in the city might alert him, and our swords will suffice, though perhaps some spears hidden away at the end of the street where I will be standing might be useful."

"Why do you believe this street would be the best?"

"It is the closest to the Palace, which will be helpful if we need to call for the guard on patrol. Angelica's drawing powder will call him wherever we are placed, but the closer to the Palace, the better for us."

"Very well, tell Serendo what you need and where it should be left. We will dine together as the suns descend, then, with my blessing and gratitude, you will enter the city."

The business of the meeting ended and the refreshments arrived, and the conversation turned to more mundane matters, but Darius managed to pull Angelica aside.

"Not a patch on your cooking," Darius whispered. "We need to do something about that."

"Thank you," she replied, "but let's just wait and see how things go."

"I can promise you one thing," he continued, "the minute this is behind us…"

"Yes?" she asked innocently.

"Yes!" he winked.

"Ah, my wife, Princess Alexa," Prince Fenderon announced.

All conversation stopped, and everyone turned to watch the tall, elegant woman float into the room.

"Welcome to the Principality of Zanderone," she said looking directly at Angelica. "Thank you for coming to help us. We have been in a terrible state."

"It is an honor and a privilege," Angelica said as she curtsied.

"Lizbett, how good to see you again. Larian and Darius, our mighty warriors. We are so grateful that you are willing to carry out this dangerous mission."

"We pray for success," Darius said bowing his head, "and I believe the mission is far less dangerous with Angelica's magic to help us."

"I believe he is right," the Prince interjected, "but on to other matters. Since Larian and Darius must stay to discuss the new warrior recruits, my wife has suggested Angelica might like a tour of the Palace, and I believe there are some areas you have yet to see, Princess Lizbett."

"That would be wonderful," Angelica beamed. "Thank you."

"Lizbett, would you care to join us?" Alexa asked.

"I most certainly would," she nodded.

"Then we shall say goodbye to our men," Prince Alexa smiled, "and spend the afternoon on a leisurely stroll. I am looking forward to showing you the gardens. They are exquisite."

"Do you have herbs growing there?" Angelica asked.

"Many. Perhaps you can enlighten me as to their uses."

"It would my pleasure," Angelica smiled.

They headed out, and Darius and Larian shared a look. The afternoon would soon pass, the suns would descend, the moons would rise, and with Angelica at their side, they would soon be in the shadows of the city seeking a killer.

CHAPTER SEVENTEEN

When Lizbett and Angelica returned from their afternoon with Princess Alexa, they found their warriors waiting for them in the salon of Lizbett and Larian's luxurious apartment. The tour of the Palace and the gardens had been fun and fascinating, but tiring, and both girls wanted to rest before dinner. Angelica left with Darius to return to her room, and Lizbett dropped on her bed, pulled off her shoes, and fell backwards.

"I am all walked out," she moaned.

"Just as well you won't be with us tonight, you look exhausted," Larian remarked as he sat on the bed next to her.

"I am. This Palace is amazing. The library, so many books, and the gardens, my goodness. Angelica had both Alexa and me standing there absolutely in awe. She knew every herb, their medicinal uses, how you should use them in cooking, everything. She said many of them had magical properties. Honestly, Larian, she is remarkable. I can't even begin to think of myself as a witch after seeing her do that this afternoon."

"You carry the gene so you are one, you're just not practicing."

"I guess," she sighed.

"Was Alexa nervous around her?"

"At first, but Angelica was so friendly and so normal I think Alexa forgot until Angelica started talking about the herbs, and then she was so interested it sort of, pushed the fear away."

"I would have enjoyed listening to Angelica myself," Larian remarked.

"Larian, would you please lay down with me?" Lizbett bleated. "I need you to hold me."

"Of course," he smiled, and pulling off his boots he stretched out next to her.

"We have to change for dinner soon," she yawned. "I'm starving, but so tired. I wish we could just lay here through the passage of the moons."

"That would be a lovely thing to do," he murmured pulling her into his chest.

"I hope your plan works and you capture this evil man quickly. The Prince wants you to bring him in alive, doesn't he?"

"Yes, he does. From Angelica's vision we're sure he's from the group that tried to settle here, so it's important to learn if there are others with him."

"I can certainly understand that," she mumbled.

"Poor girl. You really are weary."

"I am. I wish I didn't have to go to dinner."

"Perhaps you'll be able to sleep after I leave."

"I won't, not with you out there and a maniac on the loose."

"You don't have any foolish ideas in that head of yours, do you?"

"Ideas? Like what?"

"Like, leaving here, following me, thinking you could help."

"My gosh, no, I most certainly do not," she declared.

"A simple no would have been enough," he chuckled. "Your protest tells me you thought about it."

"I did, kind of, but only briefly," she quietly admitted, "but I know it would be totally foolish, and now I'm too tired even if I wanted to."

"I'm going to have two of my best warriors right outside your door. No-one will be allowed in or out until I return."

"What? I can't just go for a wander if I get bored?"

"No. I understand the Palace is safe, but I'm not prepared to take any chances with you, my precious wife, none. Understood?"

"Yes, Larian, and I love you for being so protective. Will you hold me until we have to change for dinner?"

"Nothing could pry me away from you," he sighed, tightening his protective hold.

In the chamber next to Lizbett's, a similar scene was playing out between Darius and Angelica, though Angelica wanted more than a short nap in her warrior's arms. She had pulled off her shoes as Lizbett had done, and laid on the bed next to him, but her hand had begun wandering towards his crotch.

"Naughty witch," he scolded pushing it away.

"Why, can't we enjoy each other for just a few minutes? Soon we will have to go to dinner, and then out into the dark city."

"I do not wish to drain my energy, and I do not wish to drain yours either. You're already tired, I can see it, and when I am with you for the first time, it will not be hurried. I intend to absolutely savor you."

"But, Darius, couldn't we just-"

"Stop it. I don't want to spank you, but I will if you don't behave."

"You're not fair," she grumbled.

"What a spoilt child you sound like at times. You said the same thing at your cottage, and I think I made the same remark then. Perhaps I should spank you. That would settle you down."

"It would, but it would also make me feel other things as well," she purred gazing up at him.

"I think I'm going to climb off this bed and let you nap alone."

"No, please don't leave, I promise I'll be good."

"That maybe so, but laying with you like this, all I want to do is take off my clothes, then take off yours. I really do think it would be better if I went into my own chamber until it's time to join the Prince for dinner."

"Ugh. So not fair!"

"There you go again," he chuckled sitting up. "Angelica, I really do need to focus, and being with you…it's not helping."

"Okay," she sighed. "Maybe you're right."

"I'll knock on your door when it's time to get ready," he promised as he rose from the bed. "Do you have a change of clothes?"

"Yes, Lizbett has lent me some things."

"Good. You get some rest."

He kissed her on the forehead and ambled across to the door that would take him to his own rooms, but turned and looked back at her before leaving. Her eyes were already closed.

You are too tired. I hope you'll be rejuvenated for our work tonight. You'll need to be sharp.

In his room he stripped off and laid on his bed. His cock was urgently asking for attention, and as he rubbed himself he imagined Angelica sitting astride him, riding his cock as he busied his fingers with her nipples.

Yes, I will have you do that. I will slap your thighs, and reach around to smack your bottom as you bounce, and bounce you will my lovely. You will bounce on my stiff rod until I flip you over and plunge into you and make you scream your joy.

His mighty cock bubbled into his hand as the prickling convulsions began shooting through his limbs. The warm, satisfying orgasm left him relaxed enough to close his eyes for just a few minutes. When he fluttered them open, he stretched, rose up and padded to the anteroom to wash up.

Larian and I soon will be out on the streets. We have fought many battles together, but never one like this. I pray the two moons will bless our mission, and bring us back safely to our women.

Curled up in a cluster of rocks at a nearby river, Lokai was waking from a deep sleep. Had anyone passed they may not have even noticed him. The grey color of his skin blended against his hard bed, and his long stringy hair looked like algae.

Though he would move about in the shadows during the day, he was a nocturnal creature. The suns didn't like him. They made him weak, but when the moons slowly lifted into the sky he would feel the strength return to his body, and his mind would clear.

He was carnivorous, and could eat raw or cooked meat. He preferred raw, and had been enjoying an excellent diet stealing from the local meat sellers in the city, though there had been one night when a group of merchants patrolling their neighborhood had been a nuisance.

He had cackled as he'd watched their foolish attempts at guarding the businesses that lined the lane, and he'd even followed them for a time, thinking he might kill them all, but there were too many, and the ones watching would scream.

It was the shocked expressions on the faces of his victims that he enjoyed the most, even more than the killing itself.

As he would squat down, his knees separated and his long arms resting in front of him, they would stare at him with a puzzled frown. Then his eyelids would shift back, his bulbous eyes would inflate, and he would spring, covering the distance between himself and his victim in a single, huge bound. They rarely had time to react.

The arrival of the noble carriage accompanied by the Zanderonian warriors had told him someone important had arrived at the Palace. He had learned that visiting dignitaries were housed on the third floor of the main building, and the Prince's apartments were beneath them on the second floor. His initial plan had been to locate the Prince and Princess and hold them hostage until his demands were met, then kill them and take over the Palace, but he was reconsidering. Visiting nobles might be even more advantageous.

Tall and thin, Lokai was almost lizard-like in appearance. His fingers and toes were abnormally long, with bumps at the end of them. When needed, the skin would slide back, like an eyelid, revealing suction cups, enabling him to quickly and safely scale any wall. Entering the Palace wouldn't be difficult, it was silently killing the guards that would cross his path that might be the challenge. A single guard presented no problem, but they traveled in pairs.

Slipping from his clothes, he padded down to the shoreline, walked into the water, and like an eel he stretched out his long, sinewy body and disappeared. His early morning and late afternoon swims were imperative. They cleansed him, fortified him, released the kinks from his muscles, and kept him alive. Without being in the water twice a day, his skin would begin to shrivel. After a single pass of the moons he would fall sick, and if he didn't return to the water quickly he would die.

His swim, mostly in the depths, would last until the suns had sunk below the hills and the moons were ascending, then he would move back to shore, allow his skin to dry naturally, and don his clothes, then he would be strong, he would be silent, and he would be lethal.

CHAPTER EIGHTEEN

Dinner with Prince Fenderon and Princess Alexa was held in a small dining room in the Prince's apartment, and though the food was well presented and served with great care, Darius glanced at Angelica more than once, silently sending her a message.

This food needs your touch.

She felt flattered, and was tempted to cast a spell to have everyone believe the food was outstanding, but she was trying to ignore the various thoughts floating around the table, and wanted to save her strength for the mission ahead.

The energy she felt from the Prince and Princess was rampant worry. Larian's energy was split between his anxiety about Lizbett and the task before him. Lizbett was barely touching her food, consumed with fear that Larian might be harmed. For Angelica it was all quite taxing, and she was relieved when the dinner finally ended.

"My wife and I wish you well tonight," Prince Fenderon said standing up to address them. "Larian, Darius, as Warriors of the First Order you have experienced many things. You are skilled and smart, you are strong and cunning. I believe this man will be no match for either of you, let alone the two of you working as a team. Angelica, your potent skills are providing a unique support. We know little about this enemy, and I'm sure your magic will greatly contribute to the success of this mission. Thank you for journeying here to help us. Our thoughts and our hearts will be with you, and we will not rest until you have safely returned. May the moons and suns and the powers of the cosmos bless and protect you."

As he and Princess Alexa left the table, Larian, Darius, Lizbett and Angelica all rose and bowed their heads, keeping them lowered until the royal couple had left the room.

"It is time," Larian declared.

It was a superfluous statement, but the announcement was needed, and as the somber mood settled around them, they headed out to return to their chambers. There was no conversation as they walked up the stairs and down the passageway, but as Angelica split off to enter her room to collect her pouch, she paused.

"Wait," she said abruptly. "I am feeling something."

"What is it?" Larius asked anxiously.

"He is close," she said turning to face them, her deep purple eyes growing cloudy. "We must be very careful leaving the castle. Yes, he is very close."

"While you are collecting your things I'll pull the cord for Serendo," Larian said grimly. "He may be able to give us a more covert means of leaving the Palace."

"I'm going to collect my hand knife," Darius declared moving towards his door. "I'll be right there."

Larian and Lizbett entered their apartment, and Larian strode to the fireplace and pulled the long, thick rope.

"I'm suddenly scared," Lizbett mumbled. "I'm sorry, I shouldn't be, but I am."

"I understand," Larian said moving across to hug her. "I'm grateful Angelica is with us. She can sense what we can't see. Already she has proven how valuable she is."

"I know I'm supposed to be strong for you right now," Lizbett whispered, "but all I'm feeling is fear."

"Knowing you are here with the guards posted outside the door will give me the freedom to think clearly. You need not worry, Lizbett, your warrior will return. I promised you that when we were young, and I kept my promise, did I not?"

"Yes, you did, though it took you too long," she said managing a smile.

"I kept my promise then, and I will keep my promise now. Before the moons descend you will be back in my arms."

"You sound so sure," she sighed.

"Because I am," he said firmly.

A knock at the door suggested Serendo had arrived, and after taking a moment to warmly kiss her, Larian strode to answer it.

"You rang, my Lord?"

"Yes, please come in. We believe the man is near the Palace. Is there a secret way out of here? An exit that will keep us hidden as we leave?"

"Yes, there are two," Serendo replied. "Forgive me, but how do you know he is near?"

As he had asked, Angelica had entered through the door from the foyer.

"I can feel him," she said. "He is close, very close."

"Oh, you have a sense like that?" I have a cousin who can feel things like that too," Serendo remarked.

"Yes, Angelica is very in tune with things around her," Larian said quickly. "Darius will be here in a moment and then we must leave. Can you take us to the exit that is the most protected?"

"Of course. There is one on either side of the Palace," he replied.

"Let me see if I can feel where he is," Angelica suggested, and moving to the terrace that overlooked the city, she opened the glass-paned door and stepped outside.

As they waited, silently watching her, Darius entered from the hallway.

"What's happening?" he asked moving forward to join them.

"Angelica can feel our prey close to the Palace," Larian replied. "She's trying to sense where he might be so we can leave unseen."

"I'm very glad she's with us," Darius murmured.

"So am I," Lizbett quietly agreed.

Standing on the balcony, gazing out at the still, quiet city, Angelica could feel the fear. The streets were empty and the doors were locked, the residents trapped in their homes.

She had cast her invisible feelers into the air, sweeping them across the darkness, searching and probing for the man with the hateful heart, and suddenly she felt it. A shiver swept through her as his energy touched her, and shaking it off she turned and moved back into the salon, closing the door behind her.

"He is on the river side of the Palace."

"You look pale," Darius frowned moving across to her. "Are you all right?"

"He is cold. He is very cold. He has a purpose. I don't know the purpose, but he feels determined. I do not believe a random victim is what he seeks."

"We must leave immediately," Larian said urgently. "Regardless of his goal, we must stop him before it can be achieved. Serendo, take us to the exit furthest from the river. We will follow you."

"It's not far," he said as he headed to the door.

"Lizbett, keep strong," Larian said in a husky voice. "I love you. I will return."

Fighting the tears she watched him stride away, and as the door closed she heard the key turn in the lock. Hurrying after him she leaned against it, hearing Larian's voice as he addressed his warriors.

"You do not allow anyone in or out of these apartments until I return," he said firmly. "You must protect Princess Lizbett above all else."

"Yes, Sire."

She had barely noticed the guards as she'd come in and out, now they were very much on her mind and she was immensely grateful for them. Taking a deep breath, she moved across to the cabinet that held her belongings and withdrew her carry purse, then opening the clasp she gazed inside at the cloth sack.

"I am going to keep you close," she muttered. "I am still so scared and I don't know why. Larian is smart and powerful, and he has Angelica's magic with him. I must shake off this fear."

Pulling the sack from the bag she looped the end of the drawstring cord around her wrist, and opening the glass-paned door, she walked out on to the balcony.

The city was dark and quiet, the light from the moons muffled by cloud. A shiver rattled down her spine, and feeling uneasy she walked back inside, closed the door and drew the curtains.

Things are not right, I can feel it. I am so unsettled. I shall play with my potions. Yes, that's exactly what I'll do. I will practice what Angelica taught me. That will distract me.

Sitting down at the wide desk against the wall by the fireplace, she carefully withdrew each of the pouches and placed them in a semicircle the way Angelica had shown her. Just seeing them calmed her, and she allowed herself a small smile.

My new friends. I am glad to have you in my world.

Leaning against the trunk of a tree, Lokai gazed up at the Palace. A woman had just stood on the widest balcony on the third floor. She'd stayed only a moment before heading back inside. Now he knew which apartment to enter.

There were guards on patrol but they wouldn't be a problem. Their eyes stayed focused ahead, sometimes glancing towards the streets and avenues. Not once had Lokai seen them lift their gaze upwards. Why would they? The Palace walls could not be scaled. They were smooth, with no trailing vines, nothing to clutch for support.

The guards walked the length of the wall, turned, and walked back, and when the patrol next passed him, he would prance across the ground behind them, expose the suction cups at the ends of his fingers and toes, and begin his climb.

CHAPTER NINETEEN

Holding a flaming torch Serendo led the trio through several long passageways and some unoccupied rooms, then down a dark winding staircase. When they reached a small room at the bottom he placed the torch in a holder on the wall, and in the dim light they could make out an archway framing a heavy wooden door. The large, thick, iron handle was made to slide across, and holding it tightly in his grasp, the courtier pulled, paused, and pulled again, but it wouldn't budge.

"I don't know the last time this was used," he panted. "My apologies. I should have realized it would be difficult."

"Please, allow me," Larian said stepping forward.

Serendo watched the powerfully muscled warrior wrap his large fingers around the handle, then taking a deep breath he grunted, then pulled. There was a squeaking sound, and the bolt glided through its channel.

"I, uh, that was impressive," Serendo smiled, *and you could crush a man with those hands.*

"It was a job for a warrior," Larian remarked.

"Be careful when you push open that door," Serendo warned. "You'll find yourself surrounded by plants and bushes. They were put there to cover the entrance. It might be difficult getting through them."

"We'll manage," Larian assured him. "When you return please stop by the apartments and make sure everything is quiet."

"Of course," Serendo answered.

"Do you feel his presence, Angelica?" Darius asked.

"Not yet. I'll know better when we step outside."

Putting his weight against the door, Larian began to push. It was heavy and the hinges were tight, but like the handle it succumbed to the force of the mighty warrior. Moving cautiously through the archway he was met by a thicket of growth, but stepping in front of him Darius pulled out his hand knife.

"Leave this to me," he whispered.

Though he called it his hand knife, the blade was long and wide, and he began to slice away the stabbing, tangled branches, and crunched a path through the dried vegetation under his feet. Larian followed, guiding Angelica forward, making sure the cut boughs didn't rip her cloak or scratch her face and hands.

"We're here," Darius said softly.

Moving beside him Larian peered through the clearing in the brush. They were at the far end of the wall, and he could see the guards patrolling in the distance. Turning around he looked at Angelica. Her pale face looked even whiter in the muted glow of the moons.

"He is near," she said, "but not as close as I felt he was when I was on the balcony."

"Darius, where is the street? How far is it."

"Across the road, and a short way into the city."

Though all warriors possessed an exceptional sense of direction, Darius had amazing recall. He could study a map for a short time, then carry it like a picture in his head.

"We'll be in the open as we cross over, but then we'll have the cover of the buildings," he added.

"You go first, then Angelica and I will follow," Larian said keeping his voice low.

Moving stealthily, Darius zipped across the wide avenue, then leaned his back against the wall of the first building on the street. Holding Angelica's hand Larian followed. It wasn't far, but they were grateful for the clouds suppressing the light of the moons.

Darius crept along the edge of the building, then confidently led them through the zigzagging lanes until they reached the lane into which they would to lure their prey. They had briefly visited the site that afternoon and it had looked perfect, but in the darkness it carried an ominous feel.

"Don't worry," Angelica whispered. "He will be attracted even though it is a risky location for him."

The two men exchanged a glance. Though she couldn't read Darius, she had picked up Larian's thoughts in an instant.

"I am in tune," she smiled doing it again.

Shaking his head, Larian hurried to the dead-end. The spears he'd requested were in place, and nodding across to Angelica and Darius he slipped into the cover of the doorway.

"Are you sure you want to do this?" Darius whispered. "It's not too late to change your mind."

"I will be safe, I promise you," she said touching his arm. "Trust me."

Giving her a last, loving look, he ducked into the shadows.

Angelica stood in the center of the narrow road, opened the leather pouch tied around her waist, and withdrew one of the smaller sacks. After sprinkling its white powder in a circle around her feet, she closed it up, dropped it back into her pouch, and pulled out the metal arm band. Holding it tightly in both hands she closed her eyes and began to chant.

Owner of this band, listen, you must hear me
Owner of this band, listen, you must come to me
I am your next victim, afraid and alone
I am your next victim, far from home
Owner of this band, listen, you must hear me
Owner of this band, listen, you must come to me

You must kill another, you must kill again
I am waiting, let me know your pain.
Owner of this band, listen, you must hear me
Owner of this band, listen, you must come to me
Come now, I command it, come to me
This I ask, so shall it be.

Opening her eyes she placed the band between her feet, and reaching into her pouch she retrieved two of the smaller sacs. Carefully opening them, she held them gently, lowered her arms to her sides, and stared at the entrance to the street.

Lokai was almost to the top of the wall when he felt a strange compulsion to climb back down and hurry into the deserted streets of city. A dull thudding began in his temples, then spread through his head and into his neck. There was a victim waiting. For the first time in many passes of the moons he could sense a victim.

Closing his bulbous eyes he sniffed the air. Female. Alone. He wanted her. He wanted her badly. He needed to kill, but he needed to keep the nobles in the apartment alive.

The conflict was becoming almost impossible to bear. He ached to run to the waiting victim in the city, but he was desperate to take over the Palace. The belly of the beast was weak and vulnerable, the city was terrified and it was time. The Palace was ripe for the plucking.

Angelica could feel his conflict. He was wavering. There was another purpose pulling him away. Reaching down she picked up the armband and held it against the center of her forehead.

Sprits of the moons,
Where does he stand?
Spirits of the moons,
What is his plan?
Spirits of the moons
Why does he pause?

Spirits of the moons,
Show me his cause.

The swirling grey mist filled her mind's eye, and as it cleared she saw the Palace. A man resembling a huge lizard was clinging to the wall, and to her horror she saw he was almost to the balcony outside Lizbett's apartment.

"Larian, Darius, quickly, we must run," she called urgently.

"What is it? What's the matter?" Darius asked jumping from his hiding place.

"Larian! Hurry."

"I don't understand," Larian frowned running forward.

"The man, the killer, he's climbing the Palace wall, he's almost at the balcony of your apartment. He's trying to get to Lizbett."

"But…that's impossible," Larian exclaimed. "You must be wrong. No-one can scale that wall."

"Please, you must believe me. I don't know how, but he's there. He's about to climb over the top."

Lizbett was sitting at her desk, the small cloth sacks open, recalling everything Angelica had told her about each of the potions. There were so many details; the combination of herbs and how much of each, how long the effects lasted, and how to protect herself during their use. She was gazing at the confounding compound when a chill shivered through her, leaving a fresh wave of fear in its wake. She suddenly knew she knew she was in danger.

The protection spell. I didn't do it when they left.

Jumping from her chair she crossed her arms over her chest.

Cosmic guides, protect me now
Shroud me in a repugnant mist
Cosmic guides, protect me now
Your nasty smell I now enlist
Cosmic guides, protect me now

Cloak me in a bitter taste
Cosmic guides protect me now
Make this intruder's trip a waste.

Staring at the closed curtains, she knew the killer was going to enter her chamber, and she knew banging on the door to alert the guards was the wrong thing to do. Glancing across to her desk she stared at the pouches. Her heart was racing but she felt in control, as though a trance was taking hold, overcoming her fear.

Picking up the confounding compound and the blinding dust, she opened their sacks, and holding them gently she moved to the center of the room. Standing straight she let her arms fall to her sides, and seconds later she saw the movement of the handle behind the curtain. A long fingered hand pushed aside the heavy, draping fabric, and a grotesque, tall, ugly man with bulging eyes stepped into the room.

Larian and Darius had bolted through the city streets and had reached the road just in time to see someone climb over the balustrade of the balcony outside Lizbett's apartment.

"NO!" Larian wailed, and breaking into a sprint, calling to the guards as he ran, he had covered the road before Darius was even halfway across.

Serendon, watching from his apartment window, saw the panic-stricken warriors rushing towards the Palace, and immediately raced to alert the Prince that something was happening. As he left his rooms and started running down the passageway, guards began hurrying past him, their swords drawn.

Unaware the alarm had been sounded, Lizbett was controlling her terror. Her faith in the spell of protection was building, and not just because she believed in Angelica.

The ugly man would start towards her, then stop, eyeing her, then lift his chin and crinkle his nose as though he couldn't stand the smell of her.

"What is it you want?" she demanded trying to quell the quiver in her voice.

"Zanderone. I'm taking Zanderone. You will be my hostage."

"What did you say? I can't hear you. I'm slightly deaf."

"Zanderone," he shouted, puzzled by the woman's apparent calm. "I said, I'm taking Zanderone, and you will be my hostage."

"I still can't hear you," she repeated.

To use the magic potions she needed to be closer, and summoning every ounce of courage she possessed, she started moving slowly towards him.

"I am the one who has terrorized this city," he glowered, his swollen, round eyes staring at her.

"Are you?" she frowned still walking forward.

"Yes, yes, I am," he growled, "and what is that foul odor about you? I should kill you just so I don't have to smell it anymore."

She was so close she could almost reach out and touch him, and she was terrified of drawing nearer.

Why can't I feel it, Angelica said I would, why can't I? One more step, I'll take one more step.

Suddenly, Angelica's promise held true. Lizbett could detect his energy field.

There was no thought as her right arm flew up, and a mist of powder settled in the air around him. A split second later her left arm followed, and a bright, red sparkling dust flew through the air.

Lizbett watched in wonder as the first powder acted like a pillow for the red dust, and landed gently on his face. His long, thin arms began flailing in the air, and as his hands clutched at his eyes, an agonizing shriek echoed through the room, but a split-second later another wail sounded, and it was screaming her name.

"LIZBETT!"

The urgent cry of Larian's voice was almost lost in the intruder's painful howl, but it broke her from the hypnotizing moment. Spinning around she heard the key turn in the lock, and quickly running back from the vile intruder, she chanted the words to remove the spell.

Cosmic guides,
Remove the mist
Cosmic guides,
The smell I resist
Cosmic guides,
I am sweet once more
Cosmic guides,
Of this I am sure.

The door burst open, and rushing forward Larian swept her into his arms, the guards swarming in behind him, but Lizbett's voice rang over their heads.

"STOP! Larian! Don't let them touch him!"

"CEASE!" Larian yelled. "CEASE AND STEP BACK," then in an urgent whisper he asked, "why are we stopping them?"

"Because the potions are still active," she replied, "they'll be injured."

"Surround him, but stay back and wait until I give the order to tackle him," he barked. "Lizbett, what happened?" he asked pulling her into a corner.

"Angelica's magic," she said simply. "I'll explain when-"

"No, you will explain now," he insisted locking her eyes.

"Angelica gave me a set of her potions and explained how to use them. She didn't know why, but she felt she had to."

"Why didn't tell you me?" he scolded in a harsh whisper.

"I, uh..."

"Never mind," he sighed pulling her back against him, "I'm just so grateful you're all right."

CHAPTER TWENTY

A short time later Dairus and Angelica hurried into the room. With a passing glance at Lizbett and Larian, Angelica followed Darius as he pushed through the guards, and standing at his side she studied the strange looking man curled up in a ball on the floor. She immediately knew Lizbett had used the blinding dust and confounding compound, and assumed the guards had been warned to stay back.

"Lizbett has used my potions," she whispered, "but it's safe, you can apprehend him. He'll be very confused for a while. Don't expect to get any sense out of him."

Stepping forward Darius supervised the apprehension, and as the guards led him out, Darius paused to speak with Larian.

"Angelica just told me it will take a while for the fog to clear, so we won't question him until tomorrow," he said. "I'll meet you in the Prince's apartment, speaking of which, I think your courtier has arrived."

Looking across to the door they saw Serendo moving towards them.

"I don't see Angelica?" Lizbett frowned. "Where did she go?"

"I'm right here," Angelica replied. "I just wanted to collect your sacks off the desk. I have them in my pouch for safekeeping."

"We need to have a talk about that," Darius said firmly.

"Yes, we do, a collective talk," Larian agreed.

"I must catch up to the men," Darius said hastily. "See you shortly."

The trio turned to greet Serendo, who was red in the face and slightly breathless.

"My goodness, what a night," he panted. "You are all heroes, every one of you, and the Prince is eager to speak with you. Please, follow me."

As they headed down the hallway, Lizbett linked her arm through Larian's, and feeling the need for some warrior energy, Angelica moved to his other side and did the same.

"I hope you don't think I'm being overly friendly," she said quickly. "I have to get in touch your strength. I'm feeling a bit weak."

"Not at all," Larian replied. "I'm not surprised. I think Lizbett is a bit wobbly as well, aren't you?"

"I am, yes," she said softly.

They walked down the stairway, and as Serendo led them down the passageway of the Prince's apartment, Lizbett clutched Larian's arm tightly.

"I think I should sit down," she said weakly.

"Larian," Angelica whispered urgently. "I need to tell you both something."

"Serendo, would you give us a quick moment, please?"

"Of course, my Lord. I'll wait at the door."

"What is it?" Larian asked as Serendo walked ahead.

"Lizbett, you cast your first spell tonight," Angelica said in a hushed voice, "and it was under very stressful circumstances. That alone would cause you to feel weak, but you barely ate anything at dinner. Larian, she needs hot food, then rest."

"I am starting to feel strange," Lizbett remarked.

"I'll tell the Prince you must sit down when we enter the room," Larian said, "and see about getting you something to eat."

"Thank you," Lizbett sighed leaning into him.

With Lizbett holding him for support they continued on, joining Serendo waiting at an arched door. The courier knocked then pushed it open. The Prince was alone, and on a side table was a buffet of sliced roasted bird and vegetables, a small selection of breads and cheeses, and decanters of wine and hot tea.

"Your Highness," Larian said with a bow. "Forgive me, but my wife is feeling quite faint, may we sit?"

"Yes, of course, yes," the Prince said quickly. "Princess Lizbett, sit at the table, have something to drink, some food. I'm sure you need sustenance after your ordeal."

"Thank you," Lizbett mumbled.

"I'll pour you some tea," Larian said warmly leading her to the table.

"Serendo gave me an outline of what happened, but you must fill in the details," the Prince declared as Lizbett settled into a chair.

"Why don't I fetch Lizbett that tea and a plate of food, while you tell Prince Fenderon what happened?" Angelica offered.

"I'm sorry, I don't mean to cause a fuss," Lizbett apologized.

"I understand you faced that devil head on, and you were by yourself," the Prince exclaimed. "I'm surprised you're even here at all."

"She was courageous and remarkable," Larian said proudly, walking forward to answer the Prince's questions and give him a report.

"Please, tell me everything," the Prince said. "Don't leave out a single detail. How did this man manage to scale the wall? It is such a mystery to me."

"I don't know, Your Highness, it remains a mystery to me as well," he replied.

While Larian stood before the Prince and relayed the events of the evening, Lizbett drank several mugs of hot tea with honey, and with Angelica's quiet insistence, she began to eat. By the time Larian was finishing up, she no longer felt dizzy, and could feel her strength returning.

"Darius should be here any moment. I don't know what's keeping him," Larian remarked.

"Perhaps he changed his mind and decided to interrogate the man after all," Prince Fenderon suggested.

"No, I don't think so," Angelica said standing up. "Darius won't be able to get anything from him for a while."

There was a knock on the door, and the courtier sent to the dungeon to fetch Darius, entered with Darius following him. Looking quite flustered, and walking directly to stand next to Larian, Darius bowed, then looked at the monarch anxiously.

"You have something to report?" the Prince asked.

"Yes, Your Highness. My apologies for taking so long, but I was held up at the dungeon. This man, he is not a man like us. He has strange attachments on the ends of his fingers and toes. They look like tiny cups, and that is how he climbed the Palace walls. He began talking in a strange language unrecognizable to any of us, but another prisoner, a criminal named Vandero who has been charged with thievery, was familiar with it, and wished to barter his knowledge for a pardon."

"Did you bargain?"

"I said only that if he gave me the information I would take the matter up with you, Sire, and that satisfied him. He told me the man is from a tribe of people far down the river. It is a long journey to reach them, but few visit there because they are a vicious tribe. While they resemble us, they are not like us."

"He holds a cold heart because that's how he was born," Angelica quietly remarked.

"Yes," Darius nodded. "To survive, these river people must live near water, and if they do not sink into the river at the rise of the suns, and again as the suns descend, they will die."

"This other prisoner, Vandero, who gave you this information, tell him I will hear his case personally, and if he gathers any further information I will look upon him favorably. Perhaps he will be able to garner more information as a fellow prisoner than we might as an enemy."

"Your Highness, that is a brilliant suggestion," Larian remarked.

"Angelica, it is your turn. Tell me what transpired between you and Princess Lizbett. How was she able to have this river person under control when Larian entered her apartment?"

"I, uh, taught her some simple ways to use my potions, Your Highness, and she was brave enough to do just that."

"Amazing. Lizbett, I shall contact your father and mother and tell them how you were the heroine of this night, and Angelica, had you not seen fit to share your knowledge and your potions, we would have had a much different outcome. I shall ponder your reward. It must be more than mere coin. We are immensely grateful."

"It was my honor to serve you," Angelica replied standing up to offer a low curtsy.

"You are all my heroes," Prince Fenderon declared. "Please, make yourselves at home here, eat and drink, and rest in the morning. I must return to Princess Alexa. She is waiting for the news. I bid you all good night."

Lizbett rose with the others as the Prince left them, Serendo following closely behind.

"Angelica, thank you for not saying anything about Lizbett casting a spell, or being a witch," Larian said quietly.

"It is not my secret to tell," she replied.

"Lizbett, how are you feeling?" Larian asked sitting next to her.

"Still tired, but much better."

"Have you eaten enough? Do you need anything further?"

"No. Angelica has been force feeding me since we sat down."

"Then I'm taking you back to the apartment and to bed," he said firmly.

"Angelica, I am indebted to you for giving Lizbett the tools she needed to protect herself, but we will be having that talk."

"Indeed we will," Darius nodded.

Angelica felt her face flush hot, and dropping her eyes she took a sip of her tea.

"Goodnight, Angelica, thank you everything," Lizbett said leaning across and hugging her, then bringing her lips to her ear she whispered, "don't worry, we'll face them together. They won't stand a chance."

"Goodnight, Lizbett," Darius smiled. "Sleep well. You were unbelievably brave."

"Thank you, Darius, you get some rest too. You look as tired as I feel."

"Yes, it's Zinyana for me. I just want a bite to eat and then I'll be heading to my bed.

As Larian and Lizbett left the room, Angelica turned around to face Darius, and leaning towards him she softly kissed his cheek.

"Am I in big trouble, or just a little bit?"

"You think about that question," he said reaching for the carafe of wine, "and when we return to my room, you can give me the answer."

CHAPTER TWENTY-ONE

A short time later, as they walked down the passageway towards their rooms, Angelica looped her arm through his and gazed up at him

"Darius, am I staying with you? I mean, are we...?"

"Would you rather be alone in your bed?" he asked stopping at his door.

"No," she breathed, "not for a minute."

"That answers your question," he smiled pushing it open. "Please, after you."

The room was different to hers, and vastly different to Lizbett's lavish apartment which was decorated in crimson and white, with gold accents and ornate tapestries hanging from the walls.

Her rooms were softer in color, with pale pink diaphanous draperies, light mauve cushions, and cream silken bed covers.

The room in which she was standing was decidedly masculine, though richly done with dark leathers and thick furs. It was a man's room and it looked as though it had been decorated just for him.

"My goodness," she muttered. "I like this, I like this very much."

"It is typical of a room given to a Warrior of the First Order," Darius remarked.

"I need to soak in one of my compounds. Is there a tub in your anteroom?"

"Of course," he chuckled.

"I must remove any energy I may have picked up from that dreadful creature. I told Lizbett to do the same and left it for her in her drawer. I hope she managed it before sleeping."

"If you made it clear it was important, then I'm sure she would have made the effort. Please, help yourself. You'll find the tub is right through that door."

He was standing by the massive, dark wood, four poster bed, and she paused, staring at him.

"Yes, Angelica?" he said softly.

"I wish I could still read your thoughts," she mumbled.

"I'm sure. That reminds me," he said tilting his head to the side, "you said you were going to explain why you can't do that anymore."

"I will, but it has to be later."

"If that's what you feel, I won't question it, but please tell me, what made you say you wish you still could," he said moving towards her.

As he neared, Angelica could feel the fever starting to take her; the hot desire between her legs and the uptick in the beating of her heart.

"I, uh, just…"

"Yes, lovely witch?"

He was standing inches from her, and she gazed at his powerful chest and robust arms, the arms that engulfed her so completely whenever she found herself lucky enough to be wrapped up in them.

"I am longing to be with you," she whispered.

"And I with you," he said softly.

"I was wishing I could read your thoughts because, I, uh, know I'm in trouble, but I was hoping it could wait. I wanted to know your thoughts about that."

"Are you afraid of your punishment?"

"Yes, no, a bit, but that's not why I want to put it off."

"You want to tell me your reasons, so tell me," he said simply.

"It's a bit embarrassing," she murmured. "It's not the sort of thing I've ever imagined saying."

"Now I'm intrigued," he smiled.

"I don't want our first time together to be marred by a hard spanking, or being reprimanded, or some other punishment."

"You are quite right," he murmured cupping her chin.

"I am?" she breathed lifting her eyes.

"Why you kept your fears about Lizbett to yourself we will talk about later," he said softly. "After you have soaked, and I have soaked, we will explore each other. We will touch," he breathed, softly moving his fingertips over her breasts, "we will clasp," he continued, gripping her arm, "we will kiss," he whispered, pressing his lips lightly upon hers, "and we will press our bodies together. That is what we shall do as the moons pass across the sky. When we return to Larian's home, then we will discuss your behavior."

"You're making me weak," she mumbled.

"However, I will tell you this. You can have closeness without punishment, but you cannot have punishment without closeness. I will always hold you and comfort you after I have exacted my discipline."

"Darius," she said slowly, locking his eyes, "when you said that I think I felt the answer to my earlier question."

"Which is?"

"I'm in big trouble, aren't I?"

"Yes, you are," he nodded, "and that's all that will be said for now."

Lifting her arms around his neck, she leaned her head against his heart and breathed in his life force.

"My sweet, lovely, Angelica, you must go and soak, because if you don't I will lift you from the floor right now, and strip those clothes off your body."

Kissing his chest, she slipped her arms down and stepped back.

"This won't take me long," she promised, and with a sigh she turned and padded across the floor into the anteroom.

Darius watched the door close, then slowly started to remove his clothes. It had been a drama-filled night, and he flopped down on the bed to pull off his boots. Though it had ended successfully, and the killer was in the dungeon and no-one had been injured, questions remained, not the least of which was why Angelica and Lizbett had kept such an important secret.

You gave her potions, so you knew, or at least you sensed, that she could be in danger. It is a puzzle why you didn't tell us. I will give you the chance to explain, but there is little you can say that will make that excusable.

Finally naked, he wrapped a large cloth around his waist, wandered to the window and stared out at the city. When the moons disappeared and the suns began to lift into the sky, people would leave their homes and open their business, doing so unaware that their Prince was about to bring them tears of relief.

Prince Fenderon would stand on his terrace and address the populace, exclaiming with joy that the beast had been captured, and their lives could return to normal.

They would not be told that the cheers and laughter would return to their lives thanks to a mischievous young witch named Angelica. He could not have her standing next to him while he declared that their businesses could thrive again, and lovers could walk under the moons, arm-in-arm, in safety. They would not know that while the young witch could be naughty and willful, she was brave, and beautiful, and wise beyond her years.

Sighing heavily he shook his head.

"She should be praised and exalted," he muttered. "I know there is still a prejudice and fear of witches, and the Prince will hail Darius and I as the heroes, but I will find a way to reward her for what she has done. I don't know how, but I will."

He heard a noise, and looking across he saw Angelica moving towards him, a thin sheet draped around her body.

"I have prepared a special soak for you," she said softly. "It has something in the water that will soothe you and feed your muscles."

"Thank you, I will be back very quickly," he promised, and kissing her on the forehead he made his way to the anteroom.

Angelica looked across at the sleeping city, then walked around the room extinguishing the flames on the several lamps that were burning, leaving just one alive in a far corner. The moons had passed each other, and their cream glow fell through the windows, painting the air with a velvet radiance. Folding back the bedcovers, she dropped the sheet covering her body and laid down to wait for her warrior.

I have never ached for a man as I ache for you. I have never felt weak with a man, as I feel weak next to you. You frighten me, but you send great joy to my heart. I am a witch, yet it is you who has cast the spell. The thought of returning to my small cottage in the forest and being without you is one that fills me with sadness. Must I live only with the memory of the few moments we are about to share? If it is so, then it is so, and at least I will have that to comfort me. It is better to have this for even a short time, than not at all.

CHAPTER TWENTY-TWO

She watched him glide across to her, moving like a great cat, the drops of remaining water glistening against his skin. He didn't lay next to her, but sat on the edge of the bed and placed his palm on her chest before artfully fondling her breasts.

Gently squeezing, he pinched her nipples, dallied to toy and tease, then traveled his hand down her body, pausing to stroke her mound of soft curly hair before lowering his fingers into her sex. She moaned and wriggled, but dropping his lips on hers he muffled her sounds, and as he pushed his tongue between her teeth, he thrust a finger deep into her pussy.

He leisurely explored her cunt depths, seeking out the interior button that would shoot sparks through her body. As he gently pressed she clutched his back, but when he began pulling his finger softly out and plunging it back in, she broke their kiss and gazed at him longingly.

"Darius, please slide your cock in me?"

"Not yet, but soon," he promised.

Keeping his finger imbedded, he dropped his mouth to her nipples, devouring them, drawing each into his mouth before softly sucking, then withdrew his finger from her channel to tease her clit.

"Such a passionate soul," he purred as he listened to her moans. "You may be a powerful witch, but you are still a woman, a woman who needs a strong, lust-filled man, aren't you, Angelica?"

"Yes, yes," she muttered, "so much, but I have found men so weak. You are not weak, you are…ooh…"

Speech failed her as he rolled on top of her and presented his cock where his finger had just lingered, letting it rest for a moment, tantalizing her hungry, wet pussy.

Lifting her pelvis, begging for his entry, her hands grasped the bedclothes as he gradually pushed himself forward. Closing her eyes she felt herself being swept away into a blinding joy, and when he seized her wrists, sliding them past her head and pinning them against the mattress, she heard herself groan his name.

"I'm going to posses you," he growled. "Is that what you want?"

"Yes," she pleaded, "yes, please, yes, take me."

"No, not take you, I have already taken you," he murmured lowering his lips to her ear, "I said, possess you."

"Please, yes, possess me."

"Are you sure?"

"Darius, I am, I am so sure."

Releasing her wrists he rose slowly to his knees and effortlessly flipped her on to her stomach, then grasping her hips in his mighty hands, he pulled her hips into his pelvis.

"Place your head between your elbows," he said firmly, "show me your surrender."

Letting out a cry she fell forward, a fleeting self-consciousness washing through her at the lewd exposure, but as he surged his cock home all thought evaporated. He began thrusting with powerful strokes, dazzling her pussy. His large hands had her in a vice-like grip, and though she wanted to squirm and wriggle any movement was impossible.

She had felt the shadow of her bubble as he'd fingered her, but it was no longer a shadow, it was a looming balloon, and with every stroke it grew larger.

"Your bottom will be spanked often," he declared landing a stinging swat on each cheek, "and not just when you must be punished. I will spank you to keep you calm and obedient. If you wish to be my woman you will accept my discipline, is that understood?"

"Yes...Darius...yes," she wailed gasping between her words.

"I will not break you, but I will control you," he continued, his hand steadily spanking her, "and this is something you want very badly, isn't it?"

"Yes, yes," she panted.

"You have never wanted to admit that, have you, Angelica?"

"Noooo."

"Now?"

"Now, I do," she bleated, "I want it from you, no-one else, just you."

His hand returned to hold her hip, and keeping her tightly in his grasp he accelerated his thrusts, pumping his strapping cock until he felt the dawn of her moment, then he slowed to an even, leisurely pace.

"Tell me," he growled, "tell me what you feel."

"I feel a huge moment over me," she whimpered, "and I want it so badly."

"Do you understand what we are?"

"Yes, I do, and I want to be yours," she mewled. "I want to be yours completely."

"Subject to my will and discipline?"

"Yes, Darius."

"You will have my complete devotion," he continued, gliding in and out of her depths. "Will I have yours?"

"Yes, my utter devotion."

"Rise up on your hands so I may kiss you," he crooned leaning over her body.

Pushing herself up she turned her head, and as his fingers entwined themselves in her hair, he crushed her lips, consuming her mouth as he poured his heart into his kiss.

Angelica was swimming in a sea of intense, loving energy, his burning need and desire of her seeping into her soul, and she felt herself surrendering, giving herself over to her warrior.

"My beautiful witch," he whispered lingering his lips on her neck, "my beautiful, lovely witch, I will make you happy, I swear it."

"I know you will," she breathed, "you already do."

"You are my angel witch," he sighed, "and now you will know great pleasure."

Releasing her hair he slipped back down her body, unhurriedly kissing her shoulders and running his fingertips across her skin until he was again on his knees, gazing down at her reddened behind. Clutching her hot cheeks he resumed stroking, gathering speed as her moans dictated, feeling the growth of his pending release. His senses could feel her drawing closer, and as her body grew taut and she arched her back, he paused.

"Darius, please," she begged, "my whole body is tingling, please."

"Prepare yourself, now you will learn what possession is. Close your eyes and let your mind and body be free."

She heard his words but didn't know what he meant, and as his mighty cock began again, and he pumped her with renewed vigor, she suddenly felt her right cheek being pulled aside and his finger tickling her back hole. She wriggled in surprised protest, and was rewarded with a sound slap.

"Let your mind and body be free," he repeated, "surrender your body to me, surrender your heart, let yourself be free."

He paused his cock as he landed a flurry of swats, then propelling himself forward he resumed his measured rhythm, taking her to the brink, and when he touched his finger to her empty dark hole, he pushed it forward, demanding entry.

It was new and it was frightening, but his words swirled in her head.

Surrender your body to me, surrender your heart, let yourself be free.

When she opened up it was almost unintended, as though she had been taken over by force outside her own, and as his finger intruded, the orgasm that had been threatening to break erupted in an explosion of shooting sparks that set a deep, satisfying zing through her body. The palpitating spams vibrated endlessly, and she was free of her physical being, lost in the scintillating sensations that had taken over her being.

His deep groans sounded in her ears, and the fabulous furor in which she'd been tumbling began to wane. She could feel herself falling, dropping on to her stomach, then she felt his brawny body against hers. The beating of his heart was thudding in her ear, and his warm arms were wrapping her up. She felt herself drifting, falling into a deep state of peace.

"You are my angel witch," he purred.

Fluttering open her eyes she found she was facing the windows, and she could see the early radiance of the two suns lighting the early sky.

"Was I asleep?" she mumbled rolling over to face him.

"Yes, a blissful sleep," he purred, softly cradling her.

"I remember everything you said, about how we are, how you will be my devoted warrior, how you will protect me and punish me, and I remember how happy I was to hear your promise."

"Do you still feel the same?"

"I'm even happier," she sighed. "I have a feeling living inside me. I understand now, the possession you talked about. That's how I feel, possessed in a wonderful, amazing way. I feel as long as you are with me, I will be safe. I've never felt safe like this before."

"We are new," he smiled, "and there may come a time when you won't want my ownership. You may wake up one day and want to be free again, to create mayhem and mischief as you were doing when I met you."

"I won't ever wake up like that, and I don't know what you mean about mayhem and mischief," she frowned.

"Tsk, tsk, Angelica, please don't think you can fool this warrior. Those villagers didn't come after you for farming out some form of justice, did they? Speak the truth, or I shall have to turn you over my knee, and I'd rather not. I'm enjoying this quiet time with you."

"Will you always threaten to spank me when I don't, uh…"

"Tell the truth?" he finished.

"Ooh, I didn't mean to say that, it came out wrong."

"No, it didn't. I suspect you have found it easy to fiddle with the truth, but with me that's not allowed. Now answer my question."

"Okay, I confess," she mumbled. "I used to play practical jokes on people, but nothing really bad."

"Like?"

"I don't know," she moaned.

"Angelica, you'll give me an example here in my arms, or with a sore bottom over my knee."

"Okay," she grumbled. "There was this baker who would put his cakes and pies in a specific order. He was so particular, everything had to be perfect. Just for fun I'd use a confounding spell on him. When it wore off he would stare at his display and shake his head, as though he couldn't believe what he was seeing. It was hilarious."

"Not for him," Darius frowned.

"I'd do it every few days, but one of the young boys saw me watching from across the street and the baker put two-and-two together. He came out and yelled at me."

"Did he? Did he scold you, threaten you, what did he say?"

"Must I tell you?"

"You must," Darius insisted.

"He said, witch or no witch, I'm going to catch you and tan your hide. Of course he would never be able to, but I thought it best to make myself scarce for a while."

"How many other times did you do naughty things like that?"

"Why do you want to know?"

"Why don't you want to tell me?"

149

"Just because," she replied sitting up and resting her head on an elbow.

"Because you're ashamed," he smiled.

"Maybe," she sighed dropping her deep purple eyes.

"So, as I was saying, one of these days you may want to return to your carefree, naughty life. You may not want me watching over you, making you behave, loving you-"

"Loving me? You love me?" she whispered darting her eyes back up.

"Silly girl, of course I love you. Can't you tell?"

"Yes, I guess, I hoped so," she sparkled at him.

"You asked me why I can't read your thoughts," she murmured feeling a swell of emotion. "Now I can tell you."

"Why do I feel this is something quite profound?"

"Because it is," she nodded. "I can tell you now because of what you just said. I stopped being able to listen to your thoughts because we, you and I, have been blessed. We are destined for each other. We are cosmically connected."

As Darius ingested the words, a warm shiver rippled down his spine, and he could feel the goose bumps pop on his skin. He had heard about couples that were cosmically connected. It was a much sought after blessing. He'd once thought Princess Lizbett and Lord Larian were such a couple.

"How do you know?" he asked quietly.

"I could hear your thoughts when we first met, but not as clearly as most, and they began to fade. I felt so drawn to you it was scary. That's why I wanted to visit my aunt. She told me you were either a warlock, or you had been trained to protect yourself from a witch's probing, or…"

"We are cosmically connected," he finished.

"The way she put it was, the very nature of the blessing forbids it. Reading your thoughts, I mean."

"I can see why," he nodded.

"Darius," she said gazing into his glimmering blue eyes, "I won't always be perfect, I know I'll do things that will make you want to tear your hair out, but my heart will always be yours.

Please don't ever doubt that. I just have an evil twin that might show up now and then and she can be unpredictable."

"I wouldn't change a hair on your beautiful head. I am in love with all the parts that make up who you are. I am so proud and happy to have you in my life, and I will always want you at my side, no matter what."

Curling herself into a ball she nestled into his body, and as his arms came around her she closed her eyes.

"I am the luckiest witch in the cosmos, and I'm so glad you sought me out to help you."

"I am the luckiest warrior," he breathed, "and I'm just as glad that I found you."

CHAPTER TWENTY-THREE

It was a while later that a glum Darius trudged up the steps from the dungeons.

As Angelica had fallen back asleep he had slipped from the bed, promising to return to join her for the morning meal. Eager to find out if Vandero had learned anything he had hurried down to talk with his guards. It had been very disappointing.

Vandero had attempted to talk to the villainous lizard-like man, but not only had he learned nothing, he'd been attacked.

When he'd moved close to the bars separating them and quietly called out, the evil killer had jumped across his cell, put his thin arms through, grabbed Vandero's neck and tried to strangle him. The guards had burst in, but the suction cups at the ends of killers fingers were stuck to the poor man's skin. It had taken four guards to pry them off, then they in turn were attacked. The entire episode had been a disaster.

Darius had reached the top of the stairs and headed down the hallway. He was eager to speak to Larian, hoping his fellow warrior may have some ideas about the best way to interrogate the vicious killer. Stopping at Larian's apartment he knocked softly, and Lizbett answered the door.

"Darius, come in, we were wondering when you'd join us."

Looking across the room he was delighted to see Angelica. The sight of her brightened his mood, and he immediately noticed she was dressed in a long, flowing gown similar to the one she'd been wearing when they'd first met. Lizbett's clothes were tailored from the finest cloth, spun with gold or silver thread and made in fashionable styles, and though they had looked stunning on Angelica, Darius found himself preferring the soft simplicity of the diaphanous dress draping over her body.

"Darius," she exclaimed.

"Hello," he smiled moving quickly across to join her.

"Any news from the dungeon?" Larian asked.

"There's news, but none of it's good," he replied grimly. "Are we heading down to the dining room? I can tell you what happened on the way."

"Yes, please," Lizbett piped up, "and I'm glad you're here. I'm starving."

They began to head out, and Darius lowered his lips to Angelica's ear.

"You look lovely," he said softly. "Is that gown one of your own?"

"Yes, I felt the need of it. It's the only one I brought with me. I was a bit nervous putting it on. I know it's not the kind of thing I should be wearing in the Palace."

"You look beautiful in the other clothes, of course you do, but what you're wearing now...I think you are exquisite."

He saw a faint blush cross her face, and as his cock stirred he let out a sigh and rested his arm around her shoulder. As they walked down the hallway he started to give them an account of what had happened in the dungeon, but Larian interrupted him.

"You may as well wait. You're going to have to repeat all this to the Prince when we get to the dining room."

"You're right," Darius agreed. "I wish I had something better to tell him."

"Will we have to remain here in the Palace for much longer?" Angelica asked. "The man's been captured. Can we not leave?"

"You want to go?" Darius asked, surprised she wanted the leave the luxurious accommodation.

"I do. I need to be back with Spirit, and around the trees and grass, back around nature. The Palace is a beautiful place, but the energy of the city is starting to weigh on me."

"I'd be happy to go home as well," Lizbett admitted.

"Let's see what this morning brings," Larian suggested.

Serendo answered their knock at the private dining room door, and as they entered they found the Prince and Princess already seated. Greetings were exchanged, the four of them took their seats, and as they ladled the food on to their plates, Angelica opened her pouch and pulled out a small sack, sprinkling the powdery contents over her helpings of potatoes and eggs.

"Would you sprinkle some on mine?" Darius requested.

"Of course," she smiled, and reaching across she dusted the powder lightly over his plate.

"What is that?" Lizbett asked.

"A food flavoring," Darius replied.

"We are constantly looking for new spices," Princess Alexa remarked. "Might I try it?"

"Of course, Your Highness," Angelia said. "Just take a pinch and let it float over the food."

The pouch was passed down the table, Lizbett and Larian taking a sample as it made its way to the royal couple.

"My goodness, this is indescribable," the Princess exclaimed.

"It's absolutely delicious," Prince Fenderon concurred. "May we buy some from you, Angelica? I will want this on everything I eat."

"I have a limited supply here but I can make more. I just need to find the herbs."

"Angelica is a wonderful cook," Darius interjected. "I've never tasted food like hers."

"I can believe it," Larian offered. "This is fantastic."

"You have many talents," the Prince smiled.

"It's nothing really," Angelica said modestly, though thrilled that everyone was so complimentary. "It's just blending herbs."

"We must discuss this," Princess Alexa said firmly. "I wish to know more about it, and I wish my cooks to learn."

"To more serious matters," the Prince declared. "Tell me, Darius, what news from the dungeon?"

As Darius gravely relayed the story, the happy mood in the room turned solemn, and the Prince shook his head.

"Lizbett, Angelica, please forgive this unpleasant talk. Normally conversations such as these take place in closed rooms with my advisors in attendance, not over a morning meal with such charming company, but you were both deeply involved, my goodness, more than involved. Were it not for the two of you, that maniac would still be on the loose. I felt it only fair to include you, and there's another reason why you're all here."

He paused, took a sip of his tea, and leaned forward in his chair.

"I am not convinced this man was acting alone. Did he really believe he could take over this Palace by himself? He traveled so far, it doesn't make sense that he would undertake such a long journey just for the sake of revenge. It's possible of course, but given what happened with your father, Lizbett, and the recent attempt to take over his kingdom of Verdana, I'm suspicious. I have not included my advisors because I wish to keep our progress quiet. It is imperative that we get information from this man. We must know if he is truly a lone figure, or if he is working with others inside the Palace. How can we do that? Torture may yield us nothing. We've never dealt with one of these river people."

"Um, maybe I can help," Angelina offered.

"You can?" the Prince asked. "How?"

"I noticed some herbs in your garden that will loosen his tongue. With your permission, I can easily make a potion. Just stir it into his food and shortly after he eats it, you won't be able to keep him quiet. He'll be more than happy to answer all your questions, though his answers will be filled with far more information than you could possibly want or need."

"Angelica!" the Prince exclaimed. "Is this true?"

"I, uh, yes, it's a simple concoction," she nodded.

"When you finish your meal, Serendo will take you to the gardens. It appears I am again indebted to you, Angelica. Is there no end to your gifts?"

"They are the gifts of nature, Your Highness. I have just been born with the ability to understand them, and taught by those with much greater knowledge than I."

"You are too modest," he sighed, "and I am deeply impressed."

Darius felt his heart swell with pride. He wanted to hug her tightly, kiss her fervently, and tell her how much he adored her, but had to settle for a gaze of admiration, and a covert squeeze of her leg under the table.

CHAPTER TWENTY-FOUR

True to her word, when Serendo escorted her to the herb garden she snipped off a collection of stalks and flowers and took them back to her apartment.

"Please pull the cord by your fireplace when your potion is ready," Serendo requested. "How long after it has been eaten will the prisoner be open to conversation?"

"Very quickly," she smiled. "You might want to wait. This will be ready before you've even made it to the end of the hallway."

"That fast?"

"Yes," she laughed, "it's not difficult. Why don't you tell the others I'm back while I mix it up? They're in Princess Lizbett's apartment."

"I will, thank you, Angelica. The Prince wishes the warriors to be in attendance during the interrogation, so we will leave together."

As Serendo left, Angelica went to work grinding the herbs, then added some of her appetizing flavors to the mixture. It needed to have an appealing aroma, and palatability was essential if the man was going to eat it. The compound was moist, and there was no time to dry it under the warm rays of the sun, so she added some neutral powder, rolled it into a soft ball, and placed it in the center a small cloth, tying off the four ends.

Moving through the foyer that separated her room from Lizbett's apartment, she knocked gently and walked inside.

"It's ready," she smiled.

Walking across to her, Darius carefully took the cloth package.

"Thank you, Angelica. We will take this to the Prince immediately."

"You can mix it into anything savory," she said. "Find out from the guards what he ate and what he didn't, then put it in something you know he'll find appetizing. It won't work if he leaves it on his plate. Has he been given his morning meal yet?"

"No, I don't believe so. I know he finished off the small portion of meat he was fed last night."

"Perfect. Smother it across the top like a gravy. If he likes meat, he will love this. Believe me, he'll gobble it up."

"Thank you, Angelica, thank you so much," Serendo said.

"I'd love to be there. Do you think the Prince would mind me coming?" Angelica asked.

"Me too," Lizbett said walking across the room. "I definitely want to be there.

"No," Darius said firmly. "The dungeon is no place for either of you."

"I agree," Larian concurred. "This is not open for debate. The two of you will either wait here, or visit the marketplace, or do something else, but you will not be visiting the dungeons."

"But it's my potion, I want to see it work," Angelica argued.

"Would you excuse us for one minute?" Darius said politely, and taking Angelica by the elbow he moved her back into the foyer and closed the door.

"What?" she frowned.

"The dungeons are wretched, they have an ugly smell, and for you especially it would be a dreadful experience. You will be overcome by the horrible energy down there."

"I can use a spell to protect myself," she declared, her dark purple eyes challenging him.

"Have you already forgotten our conversation? Just a short time ago you said you understood how we are."

"Um, no, I haven't forgotten," she mumbled.

"There are times when you must do as I say. This is one of those times," he said sternly.

"It's not-"

"It would be unwise," he interrupted frowning at her, "for you to say it's not fair. The spoilt child will find herself with a sore bottom if she comes out to play right now. This is serious business. Do you understand?"

"Yes, Darius."

"Thank you for this compound, it's another miracle. Now you and Lizbett behave yourselves. If you go out, you leave us a note telling us where you've gone."

"Yes, Darius," she sighed.

"Good girl. We'll be back soon."

Kissing her lightly, he took her hand and led her back through the door and into Lizbett's apartment.

"To the kitchens, and then the dungeons," he announced. "Serendo, Larian and I will follow you."

Lizbett saw the discreet shake of Angelica's head, signaling they would not be joining their warriors, and as the men left the room Lizbett walked over and joined her.

"It's a pity," Lizbett muttered.

"Yes," Angelica nodded. "Darius was very strong with me."

"He was?"

"Yes, he was, but I understand. I've never seen a dungeon and perhaps that's a good thing. Have you?"

"Once. My father took me down to our castle's dungeons. He said because I would be Queen one day, it was important that I should at least know what they're like. It wasn't pleasant, but it was tolerable, and interesting in a way. Of course I don't know what the dungeons here might be like, though I would have enjoyed watching your potion work."

"He will be babbling like a brook," Angelica sighed.

"May I ask you something?" Lizbett said shyly. "If you don't want to answer, it's all right. It's none of my business."

"Ask me anything,"

"You and Darius?" Lizbett twinkled.

Angelica smiled and nodded, then stared at the ground as she broke into a hot blush.

"Last night?"

"Last night," Angelica whispered. "It was indescribable, beyond anything, but now…"

"Now what?"

"I am so happy, but also sad and worried. My work here is done, and soon Darius will escort me back to my cottage. It lies in the forest just outside a small village. I have been very happy there, or so I thought, but now I realize my happiness was shallow. When I think about how I will feel when Darius leaves me there…"

"Oh, I see," Lizbett sighed putting an arm around her.

"He said many wonderful things," Angelica murmured. "Things about the two of us, how we are united now, and together, but I don't know how that can happen. He is a Zanderonian warrior, he lives here. I haven't seen his home, have you?"

"Yes, oh yes," Lizbett nodded. "When a warrior is made a Warrior of the First Order, he is given coin and a house and land. Darius has a home as large as Larian's and mine, and quite close, just on the other side of the hill behind ours."

"So nearby?"

"The Warrior's of the First Order all live near each other. Larian told me it's because in times of war it's to their advantage. We socialize with the others quite often. The men are like brothers. They would die for one another."

"I know Darius and I are together, like a normal couple, but what will happen as the moons pass and time goes by."

"You are the witch," Lizbett smiled. "If anyone has a crystal ball, it's you."

"I have no such power," she sighed, "at least, not for my own life. It isn't like me to question, or worry," Angelica frowned, "and yet I find myself doing both."

"I think," Lizbett said raising her eyebrows, "that's what happens when you fall in love."

CHAPTER TWENTY-FIVE

Darius and Larian returned in a remarkably short time. The suns had barely crossed high in the sky when they marched back into the apartment.

During their absence, Lizbett had discovered some cards in one of the cabinets and had been teaching Angelica how to play. When the door opened and the smiling faces of their warriors appeared, they dropped their game and jumped up to greet them, eager to hear the news.

"I almost wish I'd allowed you to join us," Darius chuckled. "It was the most extraordinary thing."

"Tell us," Lizbett demanded, "tell us everything."

"The man's name is Lokai," Larian began, "and you were right, he would not stop talking. The good news is, he was here alone, but on behalf of his people. They live downstream, and every few days he would send a message to them by dropping a sealed container into the river."

"It's incredible the harm one man can do," Lizbett remarked. "He single-handedly shut down the entire city."

"He did," Darius nodded, "and that was the first phase of the plan. Once he'd taken over the Palace and had the royals under control, he was convinced he could bribe some of the nobles to join him. He was probably right. Given a choice of dying or joining, even if only to play along and undermine him later, he would have been successful."

"A choice that is not a choice," Angelica murmured.

"Once he'd secured the Palace he was going to send a message that he'd seized control of the realm, and a large number of his people would have traveled up here and devastated the population, ultimately turning our good citizens into slaves and making Zanderone their own."

"That's horrible," Lizbett exclaimed.

"There would have been much bloodshed," Larian frowned. "The Zanderonian people have kind natures. They are generous and warmhearted, but they would have fought hard to keep their homes. The warriors would have been ferocious in their defense of the realm, but it's impossible to know the ultimate outcome. The river people are vicious, and the weaponry Lokai described is like nothing we've seen. Many lives would have been lost."

"Angelica, your magic enabled us to capture Lokai, and you may well have saved Zanderone," Darius said huskily, "and that potion you called simple, enabled us to learn the truth about the intentions of him and his tribe. There are no words that can express the gratitude we have for you, or the debt we owe you."

"I, uh, don't know what to say," she mumbled.

"He's right," Larian said walking over to her. "The Prince feels the same. Such a slip of a young woman, and look at what your witchcraft did."

Angelica felt a large hot lump in the back of her throat and leaned into Darius.

"It is the magic," she whispered. "I just mixed some herbs."

A knock on the door broke the moment, and Lizbett walked quickly across to answer; it was Serendo.

"Angelica, congratulations," he exclaimed as he walked in. "I'm sure you've heard what a brilliant success your potion was. It was truly astonishing. I do apologize for interrupting, but, Darius, the Prince requests your company."

"I'll be back soon," he promised, and kissing her softly he began to head out, but Serendo stopped him at the door.

"I do apologize, I neglected to pass along another message," Serendo continued. "Prince Fenderon is addressing the citizens when the suns reach the third quarter. He wants all four of you at his side. The guards are moving through the city to alert the people now."

"That's very soon," Lizbett remarked staring out the windows.

"Yes, very soon," he nodded. "Darius, the Prince awaits."

With a last wink at Angelica, Darius followed Serendo out, but as the door closed behind them Larian saw Angelica didn't look happy at all.

"Lizbett," he said softly, "pour us some wine and place it on the table by the couch."

Following his gaze, Lizbett saw Angelica's furrowed brow and immediately went to the drinks cupboard.

"It's all a bit overwhelming for you, isn't it, Angelica?" he said tenderly, moving over to her.

"It is a bit," she nodded. "I'm just a simple witch, and suddenly I'm supposed to have saved an entire realm? It's...yes...a bit much."

Lizbett heard the catch in her voice and hurried the wine to the table.

"I know. I should be overjoyed, and I am," Angelica muttered, "but...I...I'm sorry, Larian, I don't know how to express what I'm feeling."

"Come, sit down," Larian said taking her hand and leading her to the couch. "Have some wine."

Lizbett sat next her and handed her a goblet, while Larian perched on the edge of the table.

"You may find this hard to believe, Angelica, but I understand what you're going through. Let me tell you a little story."

"A story?" she asked looking up at him.

"Sometimes stories are the best way to explain something," he smiled. "Would it surprise you to know the first time I was labeled a hero, I felt like a fraud?"

"You did?" she mumbled.

"I did. I felt as though I didn't deserve all the praise. Another warrior had been badly injured, the enemy was all around us, and I picked him up and fought my way back to camp. The danger never crossed my mind. My only concern was getting us both out of there, and finding help for him."

"You were a hero," Angelica declared. "A real hero."

"Perhaps, but at the time I thought my actions were those of any warrior. It was my job, it was what I was trained to do, and I couldn't handle all the praise."

"What happened?"

"My commander took me aside and said, 'No, Larian, you're wrong. I have been in many battles and seen many things, and I can promise you that not everyone would have done what you did.' It was a profound moment."

"Really? After that you felt better?"

"It took a while, but yes, I did, and Angelica, I'm here to tell you not every witch would have left her home and traveled here. Not every witch would have been so kind to Lizbett, given her lessons about the potions, then dedicated herself to the dangers of hunting an unknown killer. Not every witch would have had the wisdom to find those herbs in the hundreds that are in the Palace gardens and make the concoction that had Lokai telling us absolutely everything. You are not a fraud, you do deserve all the thanks and praise you're receiving. You deserve it, Angelica, I promise, you do."

The hot lump suddenly dissolved, and as the buried tears spilled down her face, Lizbett put an arm around her shoulder.

"Is that what you were feeling?" Lizbett asked. "That you didn't deserve all the credit?"

"Uh-huh," Angelica blubbered. "You don't know me, all the mischief I caused back home."

"I suspect it was high-spirited naughtiness," Larian said warmly. "Nothing that would truly hurt anyone."

"N-no, I never harmed anyone, not really," she sniffed.

"What you did here more than makes up for anything you might have done back in your village," Lizbett said firmly handing her the goblet again.

"You think so?" she asked taking a sip.

"Let me think about that for a minute," Lizbett declared. "Let's see, saving my life, capturing a killer, preventing the invasion of a realm, and giving the Prince a way to find out everything that was involved in the plot. Hmmm, I'm not sure. What do you think Larian? Do you think that makes up for a bit of childish mischief?"

"I'm not sure. What do you think, Angelica?"

"Okay," she sighed, a small smile crossing her lips.

"Feel better?" Lizbett asked giving her a squeeze.

"Much, thank you."

"You are family now," Larian said warmly. "You are a sister to Lizbett and to me, and we are immensely proud of you."

A short distance away on the second floor, in a private chamber in the Prince's apartment, as Larian and Lizbett had been talking with Angelica, Darius had been listening in rapt attention to Prince Fenderon.

"So, Darius, do you think this reward will appeal to Angelica?"

"It is most generous, Your Highness, but as you have learned, Angelica is a young woman with her own mind, and I am still learning what it is she values."

"I may not be a warlock," the Prince said soberly, "but I do believe I have an ability to read people. If it is not of value to her, I suspect our talented witch would have an easier time refusing you, than me. She must be thrilled with her reward, not feel squeamish about it."

"I agree, Sire. If you wish me to represent you on this matter, I would be honored."

"I not only wish you to represent me, Darius, but if the reward is not something she embraces, I give you permission to learn what she would like, and you may agree to it, whatever it is."

"Again, I must say, you are most generous."

"Darius, I would also say to you, thank you for seeking her out, for bringing her here safely. There are many in this realm and outside of it, who do not care for witches."

"I must confess, Sire, I didn't know they lead the lives they do. I met Angelica's aunt, and she has a very comfortable house and lives happily with her neighbors. It's a pity witches are still misunderstood by many."

"Indeed," the Prince sighed, "and now, Darius, it is almost time for me to address the citizens. Serendo will call for you and bring you to the terrace. Please speak with Angelica at your earliest opportunity. I will be waiting for her response."

Darius bowed solemnly, and as headed back to Lizbett's apartment his thoughts were spinning.

This could not be better. She will be thrilled...won't she? That I doubt this tells me I still know so little of her, or perhaps so little of my faith in my own instincts when it comes to her. She is unpredictable, she is unique, she is her own person, and of course these are qualities I treasure in her. I believe she will be very happy, yes, I do. No, I don't believe it, I just hope it.

CHAPTER TWENTY-SIX

When Darius entered the apartment he found Angelica laughing with Larian and Lizbett. She looked much brighter than when he'd left, and walking over to join them he saw the wine on the table.

"Are we celebrating?" he grinned.

"Yes, we are," Angelica giggled, "and I may have had just a teensy weensy bit too much of this lovely drink."

"Oh, dear, and we will be standing on the terrace with the Prince shortly," he declared.

"I'm sure you can hold her up if need be," Larian chuckled.

"I'm sure, but I'd rather not have to. I wish I could join you all, but I need to speak with Angelica privately for a few minutes."

"You do? Right now?" she asked taking another sip.

"Yes, right now. Put your goblet down and come with me. It won't be long before Serendo will be knocking on that door to take us to the terrace, and this can't wait."

"All right," she smiled tilting her head and gazing up at him. "My handsome warrior, I will do what you say. I must. It is how we are."

"Are you being silly?" he grinned.

"Perhaps, but that's how I'm feeling."

"Me too," Lizbett giggled. "Can't you have that private word with all of us?"

"No, but I think perhaps Larian might want to have his own private word with you," he winked, and taking Angelica's hand he led her through to her room.

"Alone at last," she sighed as he closed the door, and curling her arms around his neck she pressed her body against him. "I want my warrior to ravage me. Mmmm, you're so big and strong. Lift me up, take to bed."

"Angelica, behave," he chuckled trying to disengage from her limbs. "I must speak with you."

"You are speaking to me, but I don't want your words. Speak to me with your hands, and your lips and-OW!"

His hand had swatted down landing a sharp smack, and she jumped back, her eyes blazing.

"Why did you do that?"

"You know exactly why, and now I have your attention."

"Oww," she grumbled rubbing her sore cheek.

"Do you want me to smack the other side, or are you ready to listen to me now?"

"Yes, Darius, I'm ready," she frowned.

"Good. Come and sit with me," he said walking to a small settee.

"What's all this about?" she asked sitting down with him.

"Prince Fenderon has asked me to tell you about your reward. He would have done this himself, but he didn't want you to feel any pressure. You can ask for something else if you wish. Understand?"

"Sure. If I don't like it, I can say, give me a turnip, or whatever. Even a witch can understand that."

"You're being obnoxious, now behave."

"Sorry," she mumbled. "My head is starting to hurt."

"Your punishment for too much wine, but maybe this will help you feel better. The Prince is going to give you fifty dacra."

"Fifty dacra? That's a fortune!" she exclaimed.

"That's not all. I never told you this, but my home is just over the hill from Larian's."

"Yes, Lizbett told me."

"Next to it is another property, smaller than Larian's and mine, but with a lovely home. The Prince is bestowing it upon you, and will provide you with carriages and guards to move your belongings."

Angelica stared at him, as if not understanding.

"Wait, what are you saying? He's giving me a home here? Next to yours and Lizbett's? Mine? For me? My own?"

"Yes, that's the second part of the reward." *Please be happy, please tell me this is a wonderful thing.*

"I can't believe it. This a dream come true!" she breathed, so overcome she was barely able to speak. "I've been so worried about what was going to happen when this was all over. I was so upset about leaving you, or you leaving me, and going back to my solitary life. I'm just...oh, wow...this is fantastic. Is it true?"

"Absolutely true, every word," he sighed a wave of relief flooding his body, "and I'm so happy you're so excited."

"Why wouldn't I be? Of course I am."

"Why wouldn't you be? I can't imagine," he said shaking his head, *and why did I doubt this, even for a second?* "There's one more thing, and the Prince wanted me to make it very clear that you can turn this down. It is not attached to the reward, and he will not be offended or upset if you do. He has an offer for you."

"An offer?"

"He wants to set up a fully equipped workroom for you next to the herb garden. You could experiment as much or as little as you wish. In exchange he asks that teach the kitchen how to use your special spices. That would be your cover. You would be introduced as someone hired to help cooks with recipes and so forth, but you would be secretly available to him for various things as they came up."

"That sounds interesting. As long as I'm not expected to be in the workroom all the time. I could never do that. You go into the Palace often, don't you?"

"Yes, I do."

"Perhaps on some of the days you go, I could join you. Do you think that would be acceptable?"

"I do," he smiled, "and if there's anything else you want, it's yours, all you have to do is ask."

"Um, there are two things," she said. "I want to leave here right after the Prince's announcement. I want to go back to Lizbett's. I need to."

"I may not be able to leave. If the Prince wants me to stay and deal with Lokai, then I-"

"You said I could ask for anything," she insisted.

"My goodness," he smiled. "You are a tough negotiator. I suppose can always return tomorrow if he needs me. What's the other thing?"

"I would like the Prince to start a campaign to teach people that witches aren't awful. We're just like everyone else, except we have this gene that gives us a talent. We're no different from a person born with a gift for music, or the physical attributes you need to become a warrior."

"I'm sure he'd be more than happy to do that," Darius nodded. "It will please you to know he feels the same way."

"He does? That makes me even happier about everything," she smiled.

"I was very pleased to hear him say that as well," Darius said warmly. "My Prince, or rather, our Prince, is a fair-minded and generous man. It's why Zanderone has thrived."

"Will we be staying with Lizbett and Larian when we go back, or will we go to your house?"

"I would prefer my house. Both Larian and I will be entering Zinyana as the moons ascend. It would be better for me to be in my own home, and I'd love to have you there."

A soft knock on the adjoining door interrupted them.

"Come in," Darius called.

"We have been summoned," Larian declared.

"Perfect timing," Darius replied. "Everything's been settled, right, Angelica?"

"Yes, everything's been settled," she beamed.

"You don't seem to be so addled anymore," Larian remarked as she stood up and started towards him.

"I'm not," she said, *but my right butt cheek is a bit sore.*

It was a short walk to the room where the Prince was waiting, and as they entered they found him surrounded by other nobles, advisors, and members of his court. There was a table covered in food, various drinks were on offer, and young men were busy serving. The Prince walked across and greeted them warmly, then took Darius aside.

"Did you have a chance to speak with Angelica?"

"I did, Sire, and she was thrilled with everything, but she had two requests."

"Why does this not surprise me?" he chuckled.

"She insists on leaving directly after you address the citizens. I believe she is tired and in need of some peace. If you need me to stay-"

"No. You and Larian are free to take your leave. I'm still deciding what I should do with Lokai, but when I do I have others upon whom I can call."

"Thank you, Sire. The other thing she has asked, is that you start a campaign to teach the citizens about witches, that they're not so different, they're just born with a unique talent."

"I was already considering this, Darius, so yes, and I would like her help. I would be grateful for her advice and suggestions about this."

"Thank you, Your Highness. You are most kind."

"Please tell Larian, Angelica and Lizbett, that when I address the people I will be changing some of the details about what happened when you apprehended this strange lizard man. That's what the guards are calling him. A lizard man. I'm only doing this to protect Angelica."

"I'll let them know."

"Darius, I can feel something special between you and Angelica, and I want you to know you have my blessing, but I must add," he said with a grin, "I think you'll have your very powerful hands full."

"Uh, yes, Sire, there is something special happening, and you're right, my hands are already full. Excuse me, but it appears Serendo is attempting to get your attention."

"Ah, it is time. Thank you, Darius."

Returning quickly to join Larian, Lizbett and Angelica, Darius passed on the Prince's message.

"Change the details? How?" Lizbett asked.

"I think we're about to find out," Larian replied seeing the Prince signaling for them to join him on the terrace.

Sensing Angelica's nervousness Darius reached for her hand, holding it tightly as they walked out on the expansive balcony and stood behind the Prince. Throngs of people stood below them, and as the Prince waved, they cheered and waved back.

"Good citizens of Zanderone, I am happy to tell you that the killer who has kept you hidden in your homes has been caught."

There was a roar of joy, and it spread through the crowd, growing louder until the Prince raised his hand.

"We can thank our Warriors of the First Order, Lord Larian Lobergene, and Darius Dunworthy, for tackling him, but there are two others to whom we owe a great debt, and while they are not warriors like Larian and Darius, they posses the same courage and cunning. Princess Lizbett of Verdana had a friend visiting her, and this friend had brought her a gift of a strong bottle of a wine. When this fiend broke into Prince Lizbett's apartment, she didn't just get him drunk, she slipped some of her perfume into the wine. When the warriors found him he was very sick, and completely incapable of defending himself. Lizbett, Angelica, come and take your bow."

As the two beautiful young women stepped forward, the crowd cheered and clapped. The Prince's tale would make sense to the guards who had seen Lokai bumbling around, and any rumors about Angelica could be quickly quashed.

"Your lives are returned to you," the Prince exclaimed. "I have provided musicians to entertain you. Please, dance, celebrate, and go in peace."

On cue a musical troupe began to play in the town square, and the crowd began dancing, their relief and happiness almost tangible.

As they walked back inside, Angelica moved quickly to the Prince and curtsied.

"Thank you, Your Highness, for your generous reward. I don't even know what to say. I am honored to be part of your realm, very honored."

"We will talk soon, my dear. I will never forget what you did for me, for us."

As he moved away, surrounded by his friends and members of his court, Darius took her elbow and gently guided her from the room, Larian and Lizbett closely behind.

"Did you ask if we could leave?" Lizbett asked.

"Yes, and we can," Darius replied. "The Prince has given us his blessing."

"I can't wait to see Spirit," Angelica sighed. "At least we don't have far to travel."

"Thank you, Lizbett, for your kind hospitality," Darius said as they continued back to their rooms. "When we reach your home, Angelica and I will ride over the hill to my house, but tomorrow we must get together. We have many things to discuss."

"Indeed," Larian nodded, *and if Darius agrees, I know exactly where those discussions will be taking place.*

CHAPTER TWENTY-SEVEN

Climbing into the carriage for the ride home, Lizbett and Angelica were greatly relieved to be on their way with the dangerous mission successfully behind them. Sitting down with heavy sighs, they were both grateful for the opportunity to finally relax, but Angelica was bursting to tell Lizbett her surprising news. As the carriage rolled out of the Palace gates, she told Lizbett the details of her reward, and how they would soon be neighbors.

"That is so fantastic. Can I help you decorate?" Lizbett asked enthusiastically. "I've never been in that house, but I've peeked through the windows. It will be perfect for you, and there's already a big fenced paddock right next to it for Spirit, though Darius will have to build you a shelter. It only has trees."

"This whole thing is still not real to me," Angelica said. "I'm so tired, but I'm so happy. My cottage is comfortable, but it is a bit cramped. It belongs to my aunt and I'm very grateful that she's allowed me to stay there, but having my own place with you next door, and Darius right there, it's just so wonderful. I can't wait to see it. I keep thinking this is a dream and I'm going to wake up."

"I felt like that when Larian came back to Verdana," Lizbeth sighed. "I couldn't believe it. He'd been gone for so long. Somehow I always knew he'd return for me, but when he did it was shocking," *especially when he put me over his knee and spanked me, and right after we'd run into each other! That was the most shocking thing of all.*

As the carriage rocked and rolled its way home they fell into a comfortable silence, both finally able to catch their breath, and when they entered the stable yard Lizbett was so relaxed she was yawning.

Angelica however, jumped from the cab while it was still coming to a stop, and calling Spirit's name she ran across the grounds to the field where her mare was grazing. Spirit lifted her head, pricked her ears, then took off in a full gallop to meet her at the fence.

"I'm so happy to see you," Angelica exclaimed opening the gate and putting her arms around her snow white horse. "Tell me what's been going on."

Back at the carriage, Darius and Larian were still sitting on their horses, and watching the reunion, though they were amused, they were in awe of the unique relationship.

"She is something," Larian remarked. "I thought I had a close relationship with Thunder, but it doesn't even compare."

"She said she's going to teach me how to bond with Scarlet like that," Lizbett said stepping from the carriage. "I can't wait."

"Did she tell you the big news?" Darius asked.

"Yes," Lizbett beamed. "I'm so excited. I don't have any friends out here. She can teach me all kinds of witchy things, and I can show her about clothes, and running a house, anything she wants."

"The thought of you learning about spells is slightly terrifying," Larian laughed. "I'll be watching you very closely, and if anything strange happens I'll know who to blame."

"Is there anything you'd like the carriage to take to your house?" Lizbett asked.

"No. If she's left anything here we can pick up later."

"I'm going inside," Lizbett declared seeing Daphne waiting at the front door. "I want a soak and a nap."

"I'll be there shortly," Larian promised.

As the driver moved the carriage to the stables and began to unhitch the horses, the two warriors continued to watch Angelica and Spirit in the field

"Is it my imagination, or does it look as if they're having a conversation?" Larian frowned.

"No, it's not your imagination, and this sounds crazy, but they are. They have a way of talking to each other," Darius replied.

"Can she talk to all horses, or just her mare?"

"Interesting question. I don't know. I'll find out."

"There are a few things I'd love to ask Thunder," Larian grinned.

"When I left Zanderone to track down a young witch named Angelica, I never imagined, not for the blink of an eye, that things would end up like this," Darius said shaking his head. "I'm still having trouble believing it all."

"It's about time you settled down," Larian said soberly. "You are bit older than me, and forgive me, but you've been alone too long."

"There was another woman once," Darius said wistfully. "I thought, at the time…"

"You've never mentioned this before," Larian frowned. "As long as I've known you there have been many women, but always fleeting."

"I was very young," he sighed. "Minerva was her name. She was the daughter of a merchant, and I thought about her all the time. I also thought she cared for me as I did for her."

"What happened? Did I know you then?"

"You were a young recruit and you had left on one of the many training trips, I don't recall where. Anyway, one night I had a strange feeling to go to her house. When I knocked on the door it swung open, but everything was quiet, and I immediately thought some foul play had taken place."

"I would think the same," Larian remarked.

"I drew my sword, walked inside, and as I made my way to the back I heard a creaking sound."

"Oh, no."

"Oh, yes," Darius nodded. "I found her laying with another man."

"This is why you have been alone all these years? Why you have not taken a wife?"

"How foolish for a warrior to be so affected? It tore into my guts as sure as a sword thrusting through me," Darius said gravely. "I thought the injury would never heal."

"And now, with Angelica?"

"I don't know how it happened, but the minute I saw her," he murmured, "I felt something. She is restoring me. I can feel it. There have been moments when I tried to ignore it, or push it away, and you know how we can do that."

"Our ability to focus," Larian nodded.

"I did it once but it didn't last, and even this morning I was doubting, but I know in my heart I have found my home."

"This is wonderful, my friend. Now you have the joys of battling with a female to look forward to."

"Such battles," Darius laughed. "I'm not sure I'm prepared."

"Is any man ever prepared?" Larian laughed along with him. "About tomorrow, we are still agreed about how to deal with our miscreant women?"

"Yes, I think it completely appropriate," Darius said. "I will meet you there when the suns begin to cross. It appears Angelica and Spirit are ready to go home."

Angelica was sitting on Spirit's back. There was nothing around the mare's neck, no ribbon or rope, and Angelica was trotting around the field with Scarlet following.

"Remarkable," Larian laughed.

"Yes, remarkable," Darius chuckled. "I must go. I will see you tomorrow."

As Larian dismounted and walked Thunder back to the stables, he watched Darius ride to the paddock, jump off to open the gate, then climb back on. Angelica rode across to him, and sitting on their horses they leaned into each other and shared a long kiss before trotting up the hill and disappearing over the ridge.

What Larian had witnessed between Angelica and Spirit had touched him, and climbing off Thunder he stood next to his horse and stroked his neck.

"What would you say to me if you could?" he murmured. "Perhaps Angelica can tell me. Do you know I think you're big and brave?"

The stablehands nearby looked at each other, and stifling their laughs hurried out of the barn. Pulling off Thunder's saddle and bridle and slipping on his halter, Larian found some carrots nearby, picked up a few and fed them to the eager and appreciative black horse. To his surprise Thunder dropped his very large head and rubbed Larian's chest.

"My goodness. Was that for the carrots or the compliments?" he smiled, then walked him across to his paddock and released him.

Returning to the barn, he stepped into the yard and frowned at the young stable boys.

"A man who cannot show tenderness towards animals and women, is not a man. You'd do well to remember that."

He glowered at them, and watched their faces grow white before turning around and heading to the house.

As he walked inside he heard sounds coming from the kitchen, but otherwise his house was quiet. Taking the stairs two at a time, he entered his bedchamber and saw the anteroom door was closed. Tapping softly, Lizbett's voice asked him to enter, and walking in he found her soaking in the tub, various flower petals floating on top of the water.

"This feels so good," she sighed. "I am more tired than I thought."

"You've had a very scary and eventful time," he said sitting on the edge of the tub.

"I was almost asleep when you knocked. I'm glad you did or I might have slipped all the way under the water, then my hair would be wet and I'd have a terrible time getting it dry before the moons ascend."

"Do you want any thing to eat? I heard movement in the kitchen."

"Nothing. All I want is to lay in your arms and drift away. I've already told Daphne to make sure nobody disturbs us."

"I'm feeling weary too," he yawned. "I must slip into Zinyana. Why don't you come out of there and I'll just dip in quickly then join you in bed?"

"That sounds perfect," she smiled.

Helping her from the tub, he wrapped a drying sheet around her and rubbed off the water, pausing to enjoy her breasts and softly suck on her nipples, then dropping it away he gazed at her nakedness.

"You are more beautiful every time I see you," he purred.

"Please hurry," she murmured, her violet eyes gazing up at him.

"I will, and you have permission to play between your legs until I get there."

"I do?"

"A permission I rarely grant, I know, but this time, yes, you do."

"Thank you," she smiled, and turning away she padded into the bedroom.

Sinking into the fragrant water, he closed his eyes and imagined her splayed on the covers, her nimble fingers happily rubbing. His decision to allow her to touch her sex was not completely altruistic. The weariness had set in, and he knew his stamina would be lacking. He wanted to be with her, to slide into her succulent depths, but he also needed a quick end to their coupling.

Moving a scratchy sponge over his body, designed to remove a warrior's dirt and grit, he rose from the tub and quickly dried himself, and entering the bedroom he gazed at Lizbett lying on the bed.

Her eyes were closed, her legs wide apart, and her fingers were massaging the magic button between her nether lips. The sight sent his cock to life, and leaning against the wall he rubbed himself as he watched, bringing himself almost to the brink of his orgasm.

Her breath was becoming more rapid, her sounds of pleasure were growing in pitch and volume, and it was obvious she too, was nearing her release. Moving to the bed he was about to lay on top of her, but changed his mind, and straddling her thighs he rested back on his haunches.

"Open your eyes and look at me," he said, the huskiness in his voice surprising him.

Half-lidded she stared up at him. The sight of his powerful body and his hefty cock in his hand, sent a fresh wave of fire through her loins.

"Sir," she mumbled, "you take my breath away."

"Rub yourself and come for me, I want to watch you."

The instruction elicited a deep moan, and locking his aqua eyes she increased the pressure, surrendering to the hot, strong climax ready to rip through her body.

Her eyes squeezed shut, her back arched, and a deep red blush crossed her neck and chest. As she cried out her pleasure, his cock responded, and watching her fervent fingers rub her engorged sex, he groaned his response as his hot cream spewed forth and fell down his hand.

He sat back, panting, gazing at her full breasts rising and falling with her heavy breaths. Her hand had fallen away, and her pussy was slick with its juice.

I must do this more often. I will hold back as I watch her come, then take her and bring her to her moment again.

Stumbling back to the anteroom he picked up the drying cloth, and dipping it into the tub water he wiped himself clean. There was a long chain attached to the stopper at the bottom of the tub, and pulling it up, he watched the water flow into the pipe that would take into the back fields.

Moving slowly, his limbs and mind giving into the deep fatigue, he fell on to the bed, and kissing her warmly, laid on his back, his arms at his sides, his feet slightly apart.

Lizbett knew he was falling into Zinyana. There would be no further talk, and she could not lay against his chest, but just having him next to her filled her with peace. Closing her eyes, saying a prayer of thanks for their safe return, she drifted into sleep.

CHAPTER TWENTY-EIGHT

Angelica gazed around the landscaped grounds as they approached the house, and looking across the back fields she could see what looked like a fairytale house in the distance. It was yellow and white, with a high pitched roof and a low white fence surrounding the front yard.

"Darius, is that my house?"

"It is, and you can see why it has never been given to a Warrior of the First Order," he chuckled. "It would have needed major changes."

"It's absolutely beautiful," she exclaimed. "It looks like it was made for me. I can't believe it. When can I see it? Is it locked up?"

"I have the keys," Darius smiled. "How's tomorrow after our morning meal?"

"Yes, definitely. I absolutely love it," she sighed. "Why do you have the keys? Did the Prince give them to you before we left?"

"I've held them for a long time. The Prince asked me to keep them in case something happened and I needed to gain entry," Darius replied. "I knew you'd love it, and I'm sure the Prince did too. I think this entire thing is a win, win, win."

"I don't understand?"

"You won with a lump sum of money, this house, and an amazing herb garden to play with, the Prince has an incredible witch on call, and me? I have you just over the fence. Win, win, win."

"You're right," she exclaimed. "We need to celebrate, just the two of us."

"We will. Let's continue on to my house."

Riding forward she shifted her gaze to the home they were approaching. Darius had chosen a forest green color for the exterior, with cream shutters and a cream verandah that sat around the entire exterior.

As they neared, two young men hurried forward from a large barn to take River and Spirit, but as Darius dismounted he held up his hand.

"Take off River's saddle, but these horses will be living in the field next to the house while this white horse is visiting. Fill the water troughs and bring plenty of hay, and neither of you is allowed to handle this white horse. Her name is Spirit, and she is to be left alone. Understood?"

"Yes, Sir," they nodded.

"Hello," Angelica said sliding off Spirit and stepping forward. "My name is Angelica, and I will introduce you to my mare tomorrow. Once Spirit learns about you, you may pet her or give her carrots but nothing else," she said firmly, then turning around, she began moving towards the large field with Spirit following behind her like a puppy.

"Have you ever seen anything like that?" one of the boys asked.

"Never. That's amazing," the other answered.

"She's an excellent horse trainer," Darius said. "That's why you must not deal with her mare. You will only interfere with her work."

His explanation satisfied them, and while one unsaddled River, the other hurried back to the barn to collect the hay.

The bridle still on his horse, Darius led him across to the field and released him. Seeing Spirit, River immediately trotted across to join her and began showing off, tossing his head and jigging up and down.

"Men," Angelica laughed. "You're all the same. Full of ego."

"I think he's in love," Darius chuckled walking up to her.

"I think Spirit is too," Angelica smiled.

With his arm around her shoulder they wandered out of the field, closing the gate behind them, and leaving River's bridle on the verandah for the stable boys, Darius walked her into his house.

"This is exactly what I expected," Angelica smiled as she entered. "It looks just like the room you had in the Palace."

"I suppose it does," Darius agreed. "I hadn't thought about it. No woman has ever lived here so I suppose it's very, uh, manly."

A roughhewn, wooden slab table with hefty chairs sat in the center of the dining hall. In the living area the fireplace was natural stone and covered an entire wall, with large deer antlers mounted over the mantle. There were shields, swords, knives and clubs, along with other battle souvenirs displayed in various cubbyholes, and the furnishings and rugs were either brown, black or white.

"It's you," she smiled. "It could use a little color though."

"I haven't done anything to it since I moved in here, and that wasn't recently," he grinned.

"Were you as young as Larian when you became a Warrior of the First Order?"

"Not much older. Perhaps that's why we became such good friends. He reminded me of how I was when I was his age. Full of guts and grit and a determination that could not be squashed."

"You're a very impressive man, Darius," she said softly.

"You're a very impressive woman, Angelica," he whispered.

He locked her eyes, then gently placing his hands on either side of her face he softly kissed her, moving his lips tenderly over hers.

"I need to talk to you," he breathed as they broke apart.

"Have I done something wrong?" she asked. "You sound so serious."

"No," he replied taking her hand and leading her to a cowhide couch.

"What is it?" she pressed sitting next to him.

"It struck me when we walked in," he frowned. "I've never had a woman stay here with me, not even for the passage of the moons."

"Really?"

"Really," he nodded, "and I'm not sure how I'll be. If I do something that offends you, or if you need me to-"

"Darius," she murmured placing her finger on his lips, "don't worry. I'm used to living alone too, and I'm not moving in here, I moving into the house behind you."

"I know that," he said shifting uncomfortably, "but I want us to be together, whether here or in your house."

"I do too," she sighed, "but you've always been alone, and I have too, so I suppose we'll just have to figure this out together."

"I suppose we will," he said. "I've never had a conversation like this, it's very strange."

"You can't say that anymore," she giggled.

"You know what I need to do right now?"

"Yes, I do," she replied staring at him.

"Did you just read me?"

"No, I can't do that anymore, remember?"

"Then how do you know?"

"Sometimes we know things, just because we do," she laughed.

"That's true," he grinned. "So what is it that you know?"

"You want me to sit on your lap, and you want to thrust your ginormous, amazing cock inside me."

"You are exactly right," he grinned. Unfastening the flap on the front of his trousers he let his member spring free, then gripping her hair he brought his lips to her ear.

"Stand in front of me and lift your dress."

A rush of moisture flooded her sex and she rose to her feet, moved to face him, and slowly lifted her dress.

"Glorious," he muttered as he gazed at her sable bush, and reaching his hands behind her he clutched her fleshy cheeks.

"Darius," she moaned, "I'm weak. You're making me weak."

Pulling her forward he mouthed her breasts through the thin fabric, then slipped his fingers between her legs.

"Angelica," he purred, "you're already so wet and ready. Spread yourself and sit on me."

Dropping his hands he watched as she placed her knees on the couch either side of his thighs, then holding his swollen manhood, she lowered herself down.

"Yes," he hissed, "now you will ride me."

His large hands gripped her narrow waist, and he slowly moved her up and down. She moaned, closing her eyes as she relished the feel of him, and when he released her to send his hands back to her seat cheeks, she leaned forward, grasping the back of the couch for support. It took her a moment to find her own rhythm, but when she did her gasps and moans as she pleasured herself on his engorged rod sent a hot fever surging through his loins.

Clutching her cheeks he encouraged her bounce, delighting in the sight of her breasts over his face, but wanting her naked he brought her to a pause, and ordered her straighten up and be still.

"Take hold off your dress," he breathed. "I must see you."

Crossing her arms she picked up the hem, and with one swift movement she pulled it over her head.

"Glorious," he repeated in a low murmur.

As she began to resume her ride, he lifted his hands to tweak her nipples and lovingly knead her fleshy mounds, then gripping them in his hands, he pulled them to his mouth. It was enough to put her over the edge.

"I'm am so close, so close," she bleated throwing back her head.

"And you are sending me to my brink," he growled.

Releasing her breasts he grasped her waist, held her still, and surged upward with hard, powerful thrusts. She held her breath, then suddenly howled.

It sounded like the wail of a wolf, and as the convulsions shivered through her body her sugar walls clutched at his cock. He squirted his release, grunting as the intense climax rattled his spine. Moments later, when he fell out of her shriveled and spent, she collapsed into him, surrendering to the enveloping comfort of his arms.

"Welcome home, Angelica," he whispered. "I've been waiting for you for a long time."

CHAPTER TWENTY-NINE

The suns had barely lifted in the sky when Angelica awoke. Stretching and yawning she looked across at Darius, and seeing he was still in his state of Zinyana, she slipped from the bed and padded across to the window.

Looking down at the field she saw Spirit was contentedly grazing with River next to her, then shifting her gaze she saw the yellow house with the white fence.

Her house.

Looking back at Darius still soundly sleeping, she knew it would be some time before he would be up and moving around.

I must see it. I can't wait. I'll just zip over there and take a quick look.

Throwing on her dress she moved into the anteroom, splashed her face with some water, then hurried down the stairs.

The key, I must locate the key. A desk? Hmmm, I see no desk. Ah, well, no matter.

Moving into the center of the living room she raised her arms and closed her eyes.

A yellow house is waiting for me
Show me, star guides, where its key might it be
A shelf, a drawer, where does it live?
This secret, please, I ask that you give.

A white fog floated through her head, and as it cleared she saw a black lidded canister sitting on shelf. Her eyes opened and she knew it was in the kitchen. Her instinct led her down a hallway to the back of the house and through a door.

It was a large room, but it was clear it had not seen much cooking. It was clean, but the stove was old, and the pots sitting on the counter looked as if they had barely been used. Spying the black canister she pulled off the lid, smiling happily as she saw a set of keys.

Running out to the field she called to Spirit, and with River tagging along at her side the mare trotted across to meet her. Jumping on her back, Angelica broke into a canter and headed for her new house.

Stirring out of Zinyana, it took a while for Darius to realize Angelica wasn't at his side. Frowning, he slowly rose, and thinking she may be preparing the morning meal he moved to the top of the stairs and called her name. Hearing no response he walked back inside the bedroom and stared down at the field. River was alone, standing at the back fence staring across at the neighboring property.

"Naughty little witch," he grinned. "You couldn't wait."

He worked through his stretching exercises, then moved downstairs and into the kitchen. The black canister was sitting on the counter, its lid beside it.

"Of course you found the key. You're a witch," he chuckled. "Let's see what I can rustle us up to eat."

When Angelica had unlocked the front door and entered the house she'd immediately felt the energy of the person who had once lived there. It was profound and strong, and as she had walked further inside, goosebumps popped up on her skin.

The furnishings had remained and were covered with large cloths, and as she'd pulled them off she'd found charming items she could easily have chosen herself, but the feeling of the previous owner was filling her. Now standing still in the center of the living room, she paused, surrendering to its energy, and as if drawn by a magnet she turned and walked down a hallway, opening the door at the end.

Gasping, she stared in surprise at the workroom facing her. Her educated witch's eye told her what she had found.

The house had once belonged to a sorcerer.

Darius was stirring eggs near the large window that offered a view over the back field, when a flash of white caught his eye. Looking up he saw Spirit galloping towards the fence that separated the two properties. He was sure the mare was traveling too fast and would never be able to stop in time for Angelica to get off to open the gate, but moments later the horse lifted into the air. The jump had been spectacular, but the horse and rider acted as if it was nothing, and breaking to a trot they made their way to his house.

"She will surprise me every day," he muttered, and moved to the back door to meet her.

"Hello," he grinned. "Couldn't wait, I see."

"Darius," she panted sliding off Spirit and running across to him. "Did you know that house was lived in by a sorcerer?"

"What? No," he replied. "Are you sure?"

"Of course, I'm sure. It has the most incredible workroom, and his energy is powerful. I'm so excited. I wonder if the Prince knew."

"We can ask him. I doubt it. He never mentioned it to me, but maybe he didn't want me to know. Maybe that's another reason he wanted you to have it."

"Darius," she said soberly, "this was destined, I can feel it. My aunt was right. We are cosmically connected. We are meant to be together, I am meant to be in that house, though it feels like a place for me to work in more than live in. There will be times I will not wish to sleep there. I don't know why I just said that, but it's what I feel."

Her words had been earnest, and had flowed out of her like a tumbling stream.

"I'm not sure what to say," he muttered.

"Please just hold me," she said leaning into him. "Hold me."

After she had settled and her heart had stopped pounding, Angelica took over the breakfast duties. In quick order she had whipped up some eggs mixed with cheese and some vegetables she'd found in a cold cupboard, and had just enough of her spice powder to make it taste delicious.

"May I plant an herb garden here?" she asked as they sat down at the kitchen table to eat. "I'll have one at my house too, of course, but it's handy to step outside and pick off what I need when I'm cooking."

The thought of having Angelica in his kitchen stirring aromatic pots and creating wonderful meals filled Darius with joy.

"You can do whatever you wish," he said with broad smile, "and it's time to fix this house up, especially this kitchen. As I said, it's had nothing done to it since I moved in. I'll bring in one of the new stoves, and some other things as well," he added as he gazed around. "If you're going to be cooking for me you deserve to have this place right."

"Darius," she smiled, "I can cook on anything. It's about the herbs."

"Are you saying you wouldn't like new things in here?"

"Um, no, it would be nice," she admitted. "The wood on the counters isn't very good to work on, and-"

"I shall bring some workmen in from Zanderone. You tell them what you want and have it done," he declared.

"Really?"

"Yes, really," he nodded.

"I suddenly feel as if I'm about to climb a mountain," she said quietly.

"What do you mean?"

"My life has been so simple, and now I have so many things to deal with. I have to return to the cottage and organize the move of my things here, then organize the yellow house, or maybe that's the other way around," she frowned. "I to have build a shelter for Spirit in your field, supervise the building of the workroom at the Palace, and, oh, buy some clothes. I have no clothes here. So many things, Darius, how can I do it all?"

"I will help you," he promised, "except for any witchy stuff. That's your domain. You just put one foot in front of the other, take it slowly, allow everything to fall into place."

"You're right," she sighed. "I, uh, haven't actually said this, but, uh, I love you, Darius, and I'm so happy."

"I love you too, Angelica," he said softly, reaching across the table and taking her hand. "You must remember that when I'm spanking you, or reprimanding you, or we find ourselves in a battle about something."

"I will," she promised.

"Later today we can ride into Zanderone and visit some clothing merchants. I think that's a priority."

"It is," she agreed, "but why can't we go after our meal?"

"We have an appointment," he said drinking the last of his tea.

"An appointment? With who, and where?"

"We have some unfinished business," he replied.

"We do?"

"There's the matter of two young women who kept a secret from their warriors, a secret that should not have been kept," he said firmly. "Those two young women need to be taught a lesson so it won't happen again."

Angelica's heart skipped a beat, and a myriad of butterflies burst to life in her stomach.

"I, uh, thought that was behind us," she mumbled dropping her gaze to the table.

"You mean you thought I'd forgotten," he corrected her.

"Um, yes," she admitted, "I thought you had forgotten."

"Angelica, look at me."

Swallowing, she lifted her eyes.

"A warrior never forgets."

CHAPTER THIRTY

For the remainder of the morning Darius gave Angelica a tour of his property, but she couldn't focus. Her thoughts were consumed with the mysterious appointment and her pending punishment.

They were walking back towards the field where Spirit and River were grazing when Darius paused and stared up at the sky.

"The suns are about to cross," he declared. "It's time to leave."

"Where are we going?"

"You'll see. Are you wearing undergarments beneath that dress?"

"No," she whispered feeling a quiver down her back.

"Keep it that way, and please go to the house, run a comb through your hair and get ready to go. I'll have the stable hands bring the saddle across to River and I'll be waiting for you."

"Are we traveling very far?"

"No, Angelica, not far at all, now please do as I say," then softening his tone he added, "go on now, you knew this was coming," then giving her a quick hug he turned and marched towards the barn.

As he walked away she took a deep breath and stared after him.

This is so unnerving. Where could he be taking me? I could do an incantation and view it. No, I shouldn't. I'm in enough trouble, and if he were to find out it wouldn't be good, not good at all. I'll know soon enough.

Moments later Darius glanced over his shoulder and saw her hurrying to the house, but he knew she wasn't hurrying because she was worried that she might keep him waiting, she was hurrying because she was anxious. He smiled. The anticipation of discipline was important. He'd created it over their morning meal, and had marched off to build on it.

It only took a short time to have River saddled up, and Darius was mounted and waiting when Angelica appeared at the front door. She had combed her hair back off her face, tied it behind her head, and had applied her lip and cheek coloring.

Her deep purple eyes were troubled as she paused to stare up at him, but when he gave her a soft smile and a wink, her face relaxed and she moved across to the field to call Spirit. Moments later she was on her mare, and Darius began riding up the hill that separated his property from Larian's.

"Are we going to Larian's?" she asked.

"Yes, but not to their house."

"I don't understand."

"You will."

They crested the ridge and Darius turned left, taking them away from the buildings in the compound. Puzzled, Angelica wondered if he was taking her to a remote forest, but as they rode down a gentle slope she saw a small fortress ahead. Two horses were happily grazing in a fenced paddock nearby, and she immediately recognized them as Scarlet and Thunder.

I guess Lizbett and I are going to be scolded together. Makes sense. We were coconspirators.

Darius broke into a trot, and as they approached she saw Larian waiting outside to greet them.

"Hello," he smiled.

"Hello, Larian," Darius replied pulling River to a halt, but not knowing what to say, Angelica simply smiled back as she slipped off Spirit, and walked her across to the field.

"You go and play with your friends," she whispered in Spirit's ear as they entered. "Have some fun. You know everybody."

Spirit let out a soft knicker, and trotted off towards Thunder.

"Of course," Angelica mumbled. "Go for the big handsome guy. You're just like your mother."

"Angelica!"

It was Darius calling her, and as she turned around she saw River had his saddle off and was being released into the field.

"Come here, please."

Gritting her teeth she walked back to where Darius was waiting, and without a word he took her hand and followed Larian into the fortress.

Angelica gazed around the room. It was large, with a heavy wooden table in front of a fireplace. The two benches that sat on either side were as long as the table itself, and though the room was filled with other pieces of fine furniture, and rich draperies hung against the windows, she could sense the fortress had been there for a very long time.

"Lizbett, you may come out now," Larian called.

A door opened at the back of the room, and as Lizbett stepped forward it was clear she had no idea that Angelica would be there.

"Angelica!" she exclaimed.

"Please sit across from each other at the table," Larian said sternly.

Both wondering what was in store they did as instructed, then stared at each other across the expanse of the thick slab of wood.

"Angelica, why we were not informed that you believed Lizbett was in danger?" Larian asked. "Lizbett, perhaps you'd like to tell me."

"It was mutual, wouldn't you say, Lizbett?" Angelica suggested.

"Yes, it was," Lizbett nodded.

"Mutual? Explain," Darius demanded as he began circling the table.

"Well, um, when Angelica gave me the potions she didn't know was I in danger, I mean, not exactly, did you, Angelica?"

"No, not exactly."

"So, I didn't want to worry you," Lizbett mumbled.

"Angelica, did you share her concern about not worrying me?" Larian pressed as he too began to walk around the table.

"Kind of, but there was something else. I didn't want you to see the potions I'd given her, because I thought if you picked them up you'd spill them," she said quietly.

"You were concerned enough to make sure she had the potions, were you not?"

"Yes," Angelica sighed.

"Let me understand this," Darius frowned. "You got a message from the star guides, or from wherever, that you were to provide Lizbett your potions for her protection, specifically, the potions that you had brought to catch the killer. Is that correct?"

"Yes, Darius, that's correct."

"Then both of you decided that neither Larian or I should be told because you didn't want us, your warriors, the men who are tasked by their very nature to protect you, to worry. Is that correct?"

"Uh, yes," Lizbett nodded.

"On top of that, you didn't want Larian to know because you thought he'd pick up the pouches and spill the contents. Is that also correct?"

"You make it sound so bad," Angelica muttered.

"It is bad," Darius scolded.

"You think me so foolish, Lizbett?" Larian added.

"No! It was more of a joke, that last bit I mean, about you spilling the powder."

"Do you think your decision not to tell us about your concerns was sound, Angelica?" Darius asked.

"No," she sighed. "Looking back, I'm not sure why we kept it to ourselves."

"It was my suggestion first," Lizbett said. "At least, I think so. I remember saying I didn't want to worry you."

"Is there anything else either of you would like to say? You're both very smart young women. Do you understand why this makes no sense to either Darius or me?" Larian said grimly.

"You're right, and I'm sorry," Angelica sighed. "It was unwise. I honestly can't explain it, but it won't happen again."

"Good. Thank you," Darius said soberly.

"What about you, Lizbett?" Larian asked.

"Angelica's right," she said grimly. "My intentions were good, not wanting you to be concerned when you had so much going on, but we should have said something. I'm sorry too."

"You understand you must both be punished," Darius declared.

"You mean, more than this?" Angelica asked staring at him. "You've just reprimanded us, and it wasn't fun. We're both sorry, we both feel bad enough already."

"Angelica," Larian began patiently, "it's because you feel bad, as you put it, that you must be punished. That bad feeling is guilt. Until you are disciplined that guilt will stay with you. The punishment is not just to teach you a lesson and make sure you don't do something so reckless again, but to alleviate your guilt. Your bottom may be sore when we're finished with you, but your mind and heart will feel much better."

"Angelica has yet to learn about crime and consequences," Darius remarked.

"Clearly," Larian replied, "but I'm sure, in your very capable hands, it is a lesson she will understand soon enough. Both of you, kneel on the bench, bend across the table and hold hands."

Immediately Lizbett started to get into position, but Angelica sat where she was frowning up at Darius.

"I would suggest you do as you're told," he said calmly. "Do you not remember our conversation?"

"I remember," she mumbled.

"Don't you think you should be punished?"

"We just were," she pouted.

"No, you were questioned so Larian and I could make sure there was nothing we'd missed, or if there was some plausible explanation for your behavior, then you were lightly scolded. Do you think that's enough? Do you not realize keeping such an important secret could have resulted in a terrible tragedy."

"But she had the potions," Angelica argued.

"How did you know she wouldn't panic?" Darius demanded. "What if she'd spilled them, what if Lokai had reached her before she could grab them? Fortunately Lizbett kept her head, and she had the potions when Lokai entered the apartment, but any number of things could have gone wrong."

"Oh, I, uh, see what you mean," she muttered.

"If you had told us you had received a message of warning, we would have done things differently. How, I'm not sure, but we would have."

"You're right, Darius," she sighed. "I did mean it when I said I was sorry and it wouldn't happen again."

"You just don't want to be punished."

"I, uh, maybe not," she admitted.

"It doesn't work like that with me," he said firmly. "You may have been able to get away with things at your village, but that's not going to happen here, and I was very clear about that, was I not?"

"Yes, Darius, you were."

"Now, young lady, up on that bench and take Lizbett's hands. I have a feeling you like to argue just to argue. It would not be wise to make a habit of it."

Fighting her butterflies, she kneeled on the bench, leaned over the table, and wrapped her fingers around Lizbett's.

"You will both receive the spanking you deserve," Larian decreed moving behind Lizbett and raising her skirt.

Darius, already standing next to Angelica, lifted her dress above her waist, draping the fabric across her back, then moved his palm across her naked cheeks.

"We will not be speaking," Darius said sternly. "You both know what you did, and you both know you deserve this. You may yell and squirm as much as you wish, but you will not release your hands. We know exactly how long we will be spanking you, so while you can beg us to stop, it won't make any difference."

Pressing one hand against the small of her back, Darius raised the other and slapped it down. There was a pause, then the sound of Larian's hand swatting Lizbett rang through the room, and so it continued. Darius and Larius spanked their girls in a methodical rhythm with Darius dictating the pace. If his hand landed immediately after Larian's, Larian's swatting would quicken, but if Darius slowed, Larian would follow suit. If Darius dispatched a flurry of several slaps, Larian would copy him.

When Angelica and Lizbett began to squirm and shout, the men shared a look. No words were necessary. The discipline would soon be ending. They increased the sting of their blows but slowed them down.

Darius knew Angelica was reaching the edge of her tolerance and that's where he wanted her. It was no small mistake, and her debate hadn't won her any goodwill.

Larian wanted to send Lizbett a strong message. Keeping such important secrets was not acceptable, and as her bottom changed from pale pink to crimson red, and her squeals turned into a high-pitch wail, he believed the message had been delivered.

"Done," Darius declared. "Your bottom is well-roasted, just as it should be."

"It feels it," Angelica whimpered.

"What do you say?"

"Thank you."

"Thank you, Sir," Darius said firmly.

"Thank you, Sir," she repeated.

"There will be no more secrets concerning your well-being or safety," Larian decreed.

"No, Sir," Lizbett bleated, "never again. Thank you, Sir."

"You may talk if you wish, but you'll both remain where you are until you're told to move. We'll be back in a moment."

Walking outside, the warriors closed the door after them, and Larian stared at Darius shaking his head.

"You have your work cut out for you," he remarked. "Angelica is strong-minded, and let's not forget she's a witch."

"I'm not worried about her witchy ways," Darius replied. "She can't read me, and if she dares to cast a spell on me again she won't sit down for a week."

"Does she know that?"

"I'll remind her, believe me," Darius grinned.

"Wait, did you say, again? Has she already cast a spell on you?" Larian chuckled.

"She tried, but it didn't work very well."

"You're happy though, I can see it."

"Very," he nodded. "I know this will be a big adjustment, but she's worth it."

Inside the fortress the girls had regained their composure, and Angelica tried to pull her hand away from Lizbett's to rub her hot backside.

"No, don't you dare," she exclaimed. "You're right," Angelica sighed. "My instinct is to rebel, to say no, to be difficult."

"Do you want to be with Darius?"

"So much. More than I can say."

"Then you'd better get that arguing thing under control."

"We weren't very smart, were we?" Angelica muttered.

"No, but I should have known that more than you."

Angelica was staring at her, and Lizbett could sense there was something on her mind.

"Is there something you want to ask me, Angelica?"

"I'm a bit...confused," she said haltingly.

"What about?"

"I'm kneeling over a table, my bottom is on fire, and I should be furious. I should be jumping on Spirit and taking off, but-,"

"But you love it," Lizbett interrupted. "You love him, you love being with him, and you love being subject to his discipline. Makes no sense, right?"

"None! What's wrong with me?"

"I had so many days when I had those thoughts," Lizbett sighed. "This isn't the place to talk about it but we will, we'll have lunch, just the two of us, but I stopped questioning because the why doesn't matter. I've never been happier, and it gets better all the time."

"That's going to happen to me too," Angelica said. "I can feel it."

"Let's not forget, though," Lizbett whispered, "we're both witches. I'm sure we can find a way to quietly have our own fun."

"Now you're talking," Angelica grinned. "I do have another question, though."

"What's that?"

"How long will my butt be stinging?"

"Long enough to make sure you've learned your lesson," Darius declared walking back into the room. "You can get up now."

Both girls slowly moved their knees off the bench, and as Larian hugged Lizbett and led her off to the bed chamber, Darius walked Angelica outside.

"So, my sweet, adorable, lovely, mischievous witch, what do you have to say for yourself?"

"The only thing that matters," she sighed, her eyes sparkling up at him, "I love you. I love you even more now, than I did when I woke up this morning."

"You're right," he smiled, "that's the only thing that matters. Now I'm going to take you home and help you forget all about your stinging behind."

EPILOGUE

Darius kept his promise to renovate, and because the yellow house was already furnished with unique pieces Angelica wanted to keep, the items from her cottage ended up in his house. Though Darius was initially skeptical, as the transformation moved forward he started to fall in love with the new look of his home.

"I'm not feeling this way because you're making me, are you?" he joked with Angelica one day.

"Would that be a bad thing?" she asked innocently. "As long as you're happy, does it matter?"

He'd frowned at her, then she'd started laughing hysterically. In a split-second he'd lifted her over his shoulder, and spanking her all the way up the stairs and into their bedroom, he'd thrown her on the bed and ravaged her through the remainder of the afternoon.

When the workroom at the Palace was almost complete, late one afternoon Angelica found herself alone in the herb garden with Prince Fenderon. It was a rare moment, and taking a deep breath she summoned the courage to ask him if he'd known that a sorcerer had once lived in her house. He'd smiled, then nodded.

"He served my grandfather," the Prince said in a hushed voice. "When I took over the crown I was told many secrets, and that was one of them, and I was made to promise that only a talented witch, warlock, or another sorcerer would live there."

"The energy when I walked through the door was startling," she said. "I think I will be guided to discover some powerful things when I start using the workroom there."

"I think so too," the Prince nodded. "I was going to talk to you about this at some point. That house can only be inhabited by someone like yourself. We must be sure of that. Do you understand?"

"Yes, Your Highness, I do, and I agree."

"I am sure it was destined for you to come to Zanderone," he said soberly.

"It was," she nodded solemnly, "and I believe that with my whole heart."

"We will be Monarch and subject, but I also see a trusting friendship growing between us."

"Thank you. I can feel that as well."

After he left, Angelica felt a glow around her. Though she didn't know what it meant she embraced it, and as she did she realized she had finally learned to let things develop slowly, and of their own accord.

Angelica and Lizbeth grew as close as sisters. Lizbett soaked in everything Angelica taught her about witchcraft, and they spent a great deal of time in each other's homes. Angelica found Lizbett's suggestions during the renovation of the house invaluable, and to Larian's delight, Lizbett provided the kitchen staff with many of Angelica's delicious herb combinations.

When the house was finally finished, winter was beginning to make itself known, and cold blustery nights would whistle across the hills. On one such dark evening, the moons covered by heavy clouds, Darius was cuddling Angelica in front of the fire, blissfully happy.

"Darius?"

"Yes, my love?"

"Our lives are perfect."

He thought for a moment, then nodded his head.

"I hadn't thought about that, but you're right."

"Nothing is ever perfect," she murmured. "I'm worried."

"You are?"

"Yes, I am. I need to do something. If I don't, then nature will create its own something, and I need to control the something."

"What are you talking about? You're not making any sense."

"I just realized why the cosmos made me mischievous," she declared sitting up.

"I'm not sure I understand what you're saying. Could you please explain this to your simple warrior?"

"I can't, not clearly, and I'm sorry, Darius, but I have to be a bit naughty again, and then our lives will stay perfect."

"You know what will happen if you are," he warned.

"It's the price I'll have to pay. It's the only way I can ensure our perfection…being imperfect."

"You are a complex creature," he laughed. "If you say so."

"I do, so, um, just expect a bit of trouble in the days ahead."

"My goodness. Trouble? Very well, as long as you know you can expect to be over my knee," he said firmly.

"Good, now I can relax," she sighed, *and come up with something really mischievous to do. I wonder if Lizbett would like to be involved. I'll just bet she would!*

END

* * * * * *

FIVE STAR REVIEWS FOR MAGGIE CARPENTER

THE COWBOY AND THE GIRL IN THE HOT PINK CHAPS

5.0 out of 5 stars
By G Jackson
Format:Kindle Edition|**Verified Purchase**

Love the title, very catchy! If you have never read a Maggie Carpenter book then you are in for an absolute treat. Nobody writes better stories of dominant men and sassy women in need of discipline. If you are already a Maggie Carpenter fan you will be thrilled with this newest release.

THE STRICT BRITISH BARRISTER: ACT TWO

5.0 out of 5 stars
By French Cook
Format:Kindle Edition | **Verified Purchase**

What is it about a British Dominant? Maybe it's just the superior way this author depicts them. I loved this read. The series is fantastic. I thoroughly enjoyed the first book and had been waiting for Act Two.

This book is a novel in every sense of the word. It has in-depth characters and a story line that holds your attention. It has action, it has twists and turns, it keeps you guessing, and it has tons of romance, sex and spanking. Like the Billionaire series which got me 'hooked', it also has elements of BDSM, with a light touch, just enough to make you wish you were Bratty Brittany. (Or Beautiful Brittany, as he calls her when she's a good gir!!!l). Honestly, it doesn't get much better than this. Fabulous read. Thanks again Maggie

THE HEIRESS AND THE COWBOY CONTRACTOR
5.0 out of 5 stars
She knows what it's about not from reading about it but from living it, January 26, 2015
By Dwayne Garfiield (North Carolina)
Format:Kindle Edition | **Verified Purchase**

Obviously Maggie Carpenter understands what a submissive needs and how she thinks. What's remarkable here is how well she understands how a dominant thinks. So, this book, as well as many of her others, is an intense and accurate portrayal of the relationship of two people who need each other. Building trust. Handling conflict. Establishing roles and rules. I feel comfortable saying, "Perfect."

THE WARRIOR AND THE PETULANT PRINCESS
5.0 out of 5 stars
Seductive and Entertaining Adult Fairy Tale December 11, 2014
By G Jackson
Format:Kindle Edition | **Verified Purchase**

I've never been one to check out adult fairy tales until recently when a This story is sexy through and through. Though fictional, it portrays a wonderful representation of a true but loving dominant who knows exactly how to handle insubordination and defiance.

I believe the author, Maggie Carpenter, has created an epically satisfying fantasy by incorporating a bit of her own personal experiences. As stated in her author bio she is fully immersed in the Dominant/Submissive lifestyle in real life. This isn't a fantasy scribbled by a wanna-be erotica author, Maggie Carpenter is the real deal when it comes to the subject of Domination and Submission and crafts her writing in a way that delivers the psychological aspect of such relationships. I'm a fan!

I AM A DOMINANT

5.0 out of 5 stars
I absolutely loved this book, November 16, 2014
By Megan Michaels
Format:Kindle Edition | **Verified Purchase**

I absolutely loved this book!! I couldn't put it down—at all. It was intriguing to hear about relationships, and D/s in particular, from a Dom's point of view. I loved the various women and how he dealt with their needs, desires, brattiness, controlling, or defiant behaviors. The dialogue was hot and the spanking and sex scenes were breath taking. Maggie Carpenter hits a home run again, and hats off to James Collier for this sexy, hot book.

THE COWBOY'S RULES: THE SURPRISE

5.0 out of 5 stars
Cassie and Chad October 27, 2014
By Lenell
Format:Kindle Edition | **Verified Purchase**

I always enjoy reading about Cassie and Chad, they're like old friends and of course we can't forget Mickey. I love how she had Chad's horse showing in this book and Cassie's jumping. This book was HOT, hotter than the other ones I think, lots of sex and great spankings of course. Chad really helped bring out more of Cassie's submissive side in this one. Also the finally get married in this one! which is bittersweet because it probably means this is the end of their adventure. It was a fun ride!

THE STRICT BRITISH BARRISTER: ACT ONE
5.0 out of 5 stars
Sex and Spankings On The High Seas October 3, 2014
By Anonymous
Format:Kindle Edition | **Verified Purchase**

I've been a fan of this author for a while, and grabbed this as soon as I saw it. It's a bit of a departure, not because of the subject matter, or even because of the characters, the Dom is as charming and wicked as ever, and the damsel truly willful, but because the story is strictly focused on the two of them. I've always enjoyed the lesser characters in her other books, but I didn't miss any subplots or second stars. There was so much of the sexy stuff, and spanking they weren't necessary. Just one note - and I won't be a spoiler - initially I thought the characters got into things rather quickly, and I thought, hmmm, not sure about that, but don't be fooled. Ms Carpenter knows what she's doing.

THE WANTED COWBOY
5.0 out of 5 stars
Strong man, strong woman, sparks fly September 8, 2014
By Aquariux
Format:Kindle Edition | **Verified Purchase**

From the other reviews and the description, we know what this story is about, but with Ms Carpenter you never know what twists she might devise to make it sexier, more intriguing, and so much more fun to read. This is another great book, one I enjoyed from start to finish, and I'm hoping there's more to come. If you like strong cowboys and strong, independent women who have a mind of their own, this is for you.

THE HOURGLASS
5.0 out of 5 stars
They are all just great and this one was no exception January 15, 2015
By DB
Format:Kindle Edition | **Verified Purchase**

You can never go wrong with a Maggie Carpenter book! They are all just great and this one was no exception! I did have a little trouble getting into this one...Michael and Beth didn't meet until around 40% on my Kindle and it took me about three days to get that far, but man when they did, it picked up and so did I !!! I finished it in an hour or so! I would be sitting there reading and just smiling about the things they said to each and really feeling like you wanted to be her! It had more spankings after they meet than I thought it would. Even a friend of theirs met a guy and she got spanked. Loved the story, love Maggie Carpenter and it is a 5 star book!

THE COWBOY'S RULES: 2
5.0 out of 5 stars
HOT HOT HOT June 21, 2014
Anonymous
Format:Kindle Edition | **Verified Purchase**

Wow, this book is HOT. I loved the first one, and this one is HOT. There is a lot of sex and spanking, but I love how it all makes sense. All the sex and spankings flow with the story, and the chemistry between Chad and Cassie is dynamite. The other two characters, Marty and Hannah, really come into their own as well. I love Marty, he's like the big lumbering cowboy that can bear hug like no-one else, and you can really see him. I hope there's a Rules 3. (Hint, Hint). I'm thinking there might be the way this one ended. Great read. Truly great read.write a continuing story. A very happy read. Loved every page.

THE COWBOY'S SECRET

5.0 out of 5 stars
Sexy Cowboy! June 5, 2014
By Anonymous
Format:Kindle Edition | **Verified Purchase**

This book was everything I was hoping for. To have a cowboy be human was such a refreshing change, and it only enhanced his sexiness. Self-doubt plagues us all, and these bigger than life heroes are always perfect, never have worries or concerns about themselves. That's all well and good, and I enjoy their heroic personalities just as much as anyone, but to have a guy be so incredibly real - it was great. He's still strong, and steamy, and delivers spankings without hesitation, but he is plagued by his past. It's not that the woman saves him, though she kind of does, is that enough time has gone by that he is finally over the crap that happened to him. It's a great book, really great. Left me smiling and sighing.

THE COWBOY'S RULES

5.0 out of 5 stars
Very romantic and loved this book and series of Maggie Carpenter's August 15, 2014
By Anne Marie Martin
Format:Paperback | **Verified Purchase**

What can I say? Sexy cowboys in charge and the women who love/hate them! Very romantic and loved this book and series of Maggie Carpenter's. She catches the readers' attention and keeps the suspense up. Terrific scenes that make you really think that you are there as a spectator or maybe you can imagine yourself in the female's role.

THE ROCK STAR AND THE COWGIRL
5.0 out of 5 stars
ROCKED IT! July 17, 2014
By Robbie
Format:Kindle Edition | **Verified Purchase**

I absolutely loved this book. I know there are people who don't like to read about D/s relationships, but this is mild compared to other books out there. Cash and Becky are an adorable couple. Would love to see another book to see how their relationship goes. Also, would love to see a book on Sam and Marilyn.

THE BRITISH BILLIONAIRE BACHELOR
5.0 out of 5 stars
Can not say enough good things about this book!, September 24, 2013
By loveskitten
Format:Kindle Edition | **Verified Purchase**

Sexy, SO sexy.... will give you many good dreams to come! I loved the characters, it was a sexy, panty-dropping book but with a good plot! Wonderful work. I am a big Maggie Carpenter fan, for sure!

THE BRITISH BILLIONAIRE BACHELOR - ACT II
5.0 out of 5 stars
Solid D/S book with captivating plot and story, August 27, 2013
By CF
Verified Purchase

This book made it clear to me why I like Maggie Carpenter novels so much. They're not just spanking books, or D/s books. They're novels with interesting, likable characters and really great plots and sub-plots, and all the steamy fun stuff is incorporated and it all makes sense. The spanking and BDSM scenes are not just added in for the sake of them, which is important to me. I enjoy that stuff (a lot!), but if there isn't a good story for them to rest in then the book just won't fly with me. So happy to see this sequel available so soon after the first British Billionaire Bachelor. Couldn't put it down! Read it in two sittings!

THE BRITISH BILLIONAIRE BACHELOR - ACT III
5.0 out of 5 stars
British Billionaires do D/s right January 31, 2014
By Emily Tillton
Format:Kindle Edition | **Verified Purchase**

I'm going to level with you. I read D/s erotic romance for the D/s sex. Ms. Carpenter puts a great deal of plot and character around her D/s sex, and that stuff is solid, but I need to be honest and say that that's not why I'm reading a book by Maggie Carpenter. I'm reading a book by Maggie Carpenter because she writes the transition from sweet romance to D/s better than almost anyone else I know. She doesn't disappoint here: Belle (sweet submissive) and her sister Lucinda (brat) both go on D/s journeys with Simon (cultured billionaire) and Joseph (rough and tumble chauffeur) that provide plenty of hotness—especially (for my own taste) when Simon begins Belle's training. If you like young women under tables servicing the men they call "Sir," you'll love this book.

THE SPANKING PSYCHIATRIST
By Amazon Customer
Format:Kindle Edition | **Verified Purchase**

Perhaps if there were a few psychiatrists who used spanking to deal with feelings of guilt and shame, there would be a lot more adults walking around with healthier outlooks on life. My man uses spanking on me when I need it and I love the release it give me. (Not tho mention the extra bonus of the sexual arousal.

Visit the author at:
www.maggiecarpenter.com
www.MaggieCarpenter.com/blog
www.facebook.com/MaggieCarpenterWriter
www.twitter.com/magcarpenter2

PREVIOUS MAGGIE CARPENTER NOVELS

The Cowboy and the Girl in the Hot Pink Chaps
The Strict British Barrister: Act Two
The Heiress and the Cowboy Contractor
I Am A Dominant
The Cowboy's Rules: 3: The Surprise
The Strict British Barrister
The Wanted Cowboy
The Hourglass
The Cowboy's Rules: 2
The Cowboy's Secret
A Promise of Passion
The Cowboy From Down Under
The Romantic Dominant
The Cowboy's Rules
The Rock Star and The Cowgirl
The British Billionaire Bachelor
The British Billionaire Bachelor Act II
The British Billionaire Bachelor Act III
The Spanking Psychiatrist
The Billionaire's Daughter
Covert Cravings
Malibu Heat
Déjà Vu
An Eternal Flame - (*Déjà Vu–Book Two*)
Elizabeth's Education
The Inheritance - (*Elizabeth's Education–Book Two*)